To Market

Kate Ressman

GOLDEN FLEECE PRESS

Golden Fleece Press
PO Box 1464,
Centreville, VA 20122
www.goldenfleecepress.com

Special discounts are available on quantity purchases by corporations, associations, and others. For details, contact the publisher at the address above.

Kindle ISBN 13: 978-1-942195-66-5
Print ISBN 13: 978-1-942195-65-8
Pdf ISBN 13: 978-1-942195-67-2

Printed in the United States of America
First Edition
10 9 8 7 6 5 4 3 2 1

To the most important Moms in my life: Berni, Elysa, and Doreen.

Chapter 1

The Monsters on Market Street were the band that Murray's deserved. They were loud, rambunctious, and slurred as though they'd been on a five-year bender. Bianka suppressed another wince as they hit a spectacularly wrong chord. They did that sort of shit on purpose. She knew that for a fact. Their lead singer and writer, Wenceslas, had told her that over his iced tea with three sugars. They kept hoping that someone would get the joke. She looked down the scarred top of the acrylic bar to see if there were any empty glasses that need attention.

Her eyes caught on the figure of a slight woman in a glittery blue top and large dark glasses. Her platinum blonde hair was streaked through with blue and purple. She was watching the band with a frown. "Can I get you anything?" Bianka asked.

"Oh, do you have anything resembling red wine?"

Snob. "Yes." There were wine glasses on display behind the bar. What sort of idiot wouldn't keep wine on hand? It was box wine, to be sure, but it was still wine.

Blue hair nodded once, then turned her attention back to the band. Bianka poured her a glass of wine. "Five dollars," she stated. The woman put a fifty on the bar. Bianka pocketed it and reached for the change.

"Keep the wine flowing."

"Yes, ma'am." She started the tab and went back to monitoring the rest of the bar. The waitress that finally made her way back to the bar grimaced at her. She was not a small woman. She stood at Bianka's height with a round face and body that made men seem to think she should be grateful for the attention they were paying her. Her skin was a deep brown and her hair was done in braids this week. Her black tee-shirt was torn. Bianka leaned forward. "Need help, sweetheart?" she murmured into Jeannie's ear.

"I got this," Jeannie replied. Her voice was rough from cigarettes and too many years drinking. "They only ever try once." Her smile made Bianka think of sharks.

"What do you need?"

"Two pitchers of the cheapest draft and a watered-down scotch."

"All the scotch is watered down." Bianka filled the orders. "Do I need to take keys from this group?"

"They've got a double D. The poor bastard nursing his coke and looking at the bar as though it will suddenly turn into a Starbucks."

She identified the group with that description. They were next to the speakers. The poor bastard in the sweater-vest would be lucky if he could hear by the end of the night. This was obviously not his idea.

"We'll give him coffee if he's desperate. It's crap coffee, but it's hot and has caffeine."

Jeannie nodded. She scribbled the new totals on the beer coasters she used for table tabs. Blue hair-Red wine needed a refill. Bianka provided it and turned back to Jeannie. "I'll ask him," the waitress said. "Do we have milk?"

"Yes. I've got a few freaks who like milk in their scotch."

Jeannie made a face at that. She took her tray back through the disaffected mass of lingering grunge masters and sneering hipsters. There were far too many men in skinny jeans they should never have bought, women in grandma dresses and layered sweaters, and a sea of flannel that made Bianka think of high school. They came for the music, but more for the dive aspect of the bar. The old men who populated the room during the day shift disappeared right after dinner. Until about two AM it was nothing but hipsters and thirty-somethings who were revisiting their youth. After two they got the restaurant workers until about four when they closed for cleaning. Bianka checked the time. Almost midnight.

More wine for blue hair and a few more filled glasses. The Monsters went on break and the room was filled with competing conversations. Wenceslas gave her puppy-dog eyes until she poured his iced tea and sent off a round of ice water and frozen vodka for the rest of the band. The first fist was thrown at just after midnight. "Oh, fuck no." She vaulted over the bar and grabbed the offending man in a hammerlock. "Bad boy," she hissed. She "escorted" him out of the bar. She turned to the one who'd been on the receiving end of the punch. "You want me to call the cops for you?" She put her hands on her hips.

He shook his head rapidly. "No, ma'am." His eyes were wide, pupils blown by some sort of drug.

She made her way back to the scarred bar with its spider-web cracked mirror and sticky top. She frowned at the counter and pulled out a clean cloth to polish it. Blue hair-red wine smiled at her with perfectly painted blue lips. How the hell her lipstick hadn't worn off on her glass already was a mystery. Another glass of wine. She added a tick to the tab. The band took the stage again and the night wore on.

Chapter 2

Bianka collapsed onto the worn couch in her mother's apartment and immediately fell asleep. She needed to catch what hours she could before Serenity woke up. The couch was covered with a cheap grey flannel slipcover that tucked over the orange corduroy and battered foam cushions. She rested her head against the rounded arm. She woke up with a crick in her neck and her mother frowning down at her. "There's blankets you know. And there's always a pillow in the armchair. The one I use for my back." The apartment smelled like coffee and sticky buns.

"Oh, Flying Spaghetti Monster, you're baking."

"Serenity helped me with the mixing last night." Her mother smiled. Dorthea had cheerfully taken on the home ec requirements of teaching. Serenity had saved both of them when she was born. Bianka had been falling into a pattern of alcohol and drugs that would have spiraled within a few months into something unstoppable. Nate had helped stop that even before he left her pregnant with a small stash of jewelry and cash that she was sure was stolen. She kept most of that in reserve. She'd had to pawn some of it to pay for hospital costs, but still had most of it to pass on to Serenity when she got older. Dorthea had been slowing down and had fallen into a deep depression when her husband had been shot in a mugging for what little he had in his pockets. Serenity had changed that.

"Did she enjoy it?"

"She always does. Just like when you were a little girl." Dorthea's mocha skin was starting to show small age spots at her wrists and hands. Her arthritis was advancing slowly. "And we get to enjoy it now. She's still asleep. You're in luck."

"I get the bathroom. Can I borrow a shirt?"

Her mother just looked at her with pursed lips and raised brows.

"Right. I'll just go grab one." It wasn't like her mother's closet had moved.

Dorthea went to pour her first cup of coffee and fetch the vacuum. She was slowing down now. Her hip wasn't as strong. She'd busted it in a car crash about five years ago and it hadn't healed exactly the way it should have. Bianka blinked away the sudden awareness that her mother wasn't the same woman she remembered from being a child.

The shower as clean and smelled faintly like Clorox. Bianka cleaned off the sweat, spilled alcohol, and blue glitter from her skin. She looked at herself in the mirror, pinching at what little stomach she actually had. Maybe five pounds off of where she should be. If she moved up a weight class, that would be good. There were fading bruises on her stomach and chest. She made sure that the tee-shirt covered them. Her mother hated it when she showed off the bruises from the boxing ring.

"Mom!" Serenity ran to her for a hug. Bianka hugged her close. Her miracle child was seven this year. She'd gone into anaphylactic shock when they'd given her inoculations and then the treatment for the shock had triggered her again. She'd almost lost her before she remembered Nate's aversion to metal and discovered that Serenity had an allergy to most metals rather than eggs or something equally normal. "We made cinnamon rolls. And I convinced Nana that I could use the mixer."

"You were careful?"

"I didn't touch the beaters," she replied with rolled eyes that wouldn't have been out of place on a teenager. She pulled back from the hug slightly. "You didn't sneak a roll already, did you?"

"No, I'm just about to go tackle Nana for some coffee and a sticky bun."

"Cinnamon roll," Serenity argued.

"Sticky bun."

"Cinnamon roll." She bounced out into the kitchen. "Nana, tell Mom that they're cinnamon rolls."

"They're cinnamon rolls, Bee."

"Sure. Take her side in this."

"I didn't have any pecans, which is why it's not a sticky bun."

"Right." Bianka rolled her eyes at her mother. Serenity was sitting on one of the simple wooden stools at the Formica table with its duct-taped edges. It was as close to a dining chair that they'd had since the aluminum set had been sold. Dorthea was not going to have any furniture that might hurt her favorite (only) grand daughter. None of Bianka's siblings had children. The not-sticky bun was hot and made Bianka think of mornings with her father sharing his breakfast with her. He'd only gotten to know Serenity for two years before he died. It hurt that her daughter would never get to meet him. He was a strong man who'd stood up to his parents and married Dorthea despite their bullshit. Bianka couldn't stand her grandmother.

"Bee," her mother said.

"Did I miss something?"

"You were a million miles away. Want to tell me what's wrong?"

"Nothing. I was just thinking about Daddy."

Her mother nodded once. "These were his favorite."

"Grandfather liked these?" Serenity studied the bun on her plate intensely. "Even without nuts?"

"Even without nuts. Though he used to serenade me with showtunes where there were nuts." Dorthea's smile didn't seem as painfully sad. "So, what are you girls up to today?"

"We're going to the museum. Then, Seri has reading to do and some math worksheets."

"Which museum?"

"Natural history."

"I want to see the dinosaurs," Serenity stated. "And the jewelry."

"Did you want to come, Mom?"

Dorthea considered for a long moment. She looked around the apartment. "Yes, I think I would."

It was all Bianka could do to not jump for joy. She'd been trying to get her mother to leave the apartment for more than chores and church for years. "Great. We can get a hot-dog from the cart for lunch."

"And I can sit with Seri while she reads this afternoon."

Serenity giggled. "You're going to make Mom take a nap, aren't you?"

"Why yes, I am." Dorthea winked at her daughter. "I don't think she'll mind."

Chapter 3

Chester held out the phone. Bianka frowned at him. "This is Bianka?"

"Sweetie, everything is okay. Serenity had her inhaler and we were able to get to Dr. Marx quickly enough that no one tried to use metal on her. She's had a nebulizer treatment and we'll be on the way home in fifteen minutes."

"Does she need oxygen? I have a tank at home."

"We'll be at your apartment. I don't... it's just safer tonight. And I think she wants Rex-Rabbit even if she won't say so."

"Okay. I'll meet you there. I can't get off until Jasmine comes in, at least, but it's a small crowd."

"No, sweetie," her mother said sternly. "Finish your shift. We have this handled. I just thought you should know."

"Right." Bianka's stomach clenched. She needed to work hard for extra tips tonight. Enough to pay for the neb treatment and the doctor's visit. Dr. Marx had was always willing to extend them credit. She didn't have the insurance to cover all the treatments Serenity needed. "Is she there?"

"No, she's laying down with the nebulizer. No phones in the treatment rooms."

"Right. Tell her I love her, and I'll see her when she wakes up, okay?"

"Of course, I will."

"Thanks." Some impulse moved her to add, "I love you, Mom."

"I love you too, Bee. Goodnight."

Dorthea hung up before she could respond. Chester frowned. "Is Serenity sick?"

"Mom took her to the doctor for it. I don't even know what she got into this time. Mom must have taken her out to eat." It had to be direct contact with metal. Thank whoever was listening that Serenity didn't have severe cross-contamination problems, though they tried to limit that anyway. She hung up the old black phone. It was a sturdy thing from 1960 and would probably survive after the bar fell down around them.

Blue glitter-red wine was perched by the bar near the phone. She studied Bianka. She pulled out a hundred-dollar bill and set it on the counter. "No mother should have to worry about paying for her child's care," she said formally. "Allow me to assist."

"I don't need charity."

Blue frowned at her. "I have no children of my own left. Let me care for yours a little bit today."

Bianka's throat tightened and she took a deep breath. Serenity's death was a recurring nightmare. She couldn't imagine what she'd feel like if she'd actually lost her. She'd probably end up like Blue, sitting in a shitty bar and polishing off bottles of vodka not red wine. "Thank you," she said. Blue inclined her head and turned her attention back to the band. Bianka put the hundred into the little pocket she'd sewn into her bra and went back to the crowd.

Blue lingered through the disappearing hipsters. The grunge crowd held on longer and the change in The Monster's set recognized that. The restaurant crowd started to take over, filling the space with the smell of sweat, onion, garlic, and seafood. Blue's nose wrinkled up, but she simply added more fifties to her tab and kept drinking. Bianka opened an actual bottle of wine for her from the bar crew's stash and set it just below her section of the bar in recognition.

Jasmine with dark hair and a hajib didn't drink either. She wore all green tonight, covered from neck to wrists and ankles in form-fitting green accented with a gold scarf on her head and a gold skirt over her leggings. She cornered Bianka in the center of the bar near the cash register. "The private stock? Really?"

"Hundred-dollar tip."

"Okay, private stock. She's yours then. I'll take care of the idiots on this side." She frowned then. "Is something wrong with Seri?"

"Had an asthma attack tonight. Mom had to take her in for emergency treatment."

Jasmine grimaced. "Call me if that happens again. I can come in early. Any time you need."

"I don't like taking advantage."

"Any time," Jasmine stressed. "Seri's adorable. Even if you aren't."

"Ha. Ha. You're not my type, sorry, darling." Bianka batted her lashes.

Jasmine laughed. "You're mine. So that's just too bad. Though, I should probably find someone who actually believes in Allah."

"I never developed the habit. The natives are getting restless."

Her partner in crime laughed. "They'll live. She's okay?"

"She's okay. Mom's with her. And she's taking her home to cuddle with her stuffed animals." Bianka ran a hand over her short-cropped pink hair. "I'd rather be there, but I'm staying until Blue decides to leave."

"Okay." Jasmine gave her hand a quick squeeze, then turned back to her customers. She greeted her favorite regular, a short, swarthy Latino man with a face of scars. "Hey, fuck-face. How's your boyfriend?"

He snorted and replied in Spanish so dirty that Bianka almost blushed. She escaped to the other side of the bar and filled up pitchers of beer and watered-down vodka with cheerful grace. Her daughter would live another day and her smile always brought in more tips than even a low-cut blouse among this crowd.

Blue stayed until the last of the crowd was being ushered out into taxis. "Do you need a taxi?" Bianka asked her. She'd put away several bottles' worth of wine, but seemed unaffected. She was walking steadily, and her voice was calm.

"No, I am well-enough to get home. Are you off shift tomorrow?"

"I am."

"Would you meet me for coffee at the Blue-Wing cafe? I need to talk to another mother."

Bianka considered that for a long moment. She hated not spending her days off with Serenity. Her daughter wouldn't be up to leaving the house tomorrow. "Not for long. My daughter will need a nap though. Say around three?"

"That is perfect." Blue walked out without any bobble on her four-inch heels.

"Not your type, huh?" Jasmine asked as she locked the door. "Should I dye my hair?"

"It's not like that."

"Sure, sounded like a date to me." The other bartender's smile was closer to a leer.

"She lost her child."

Jasmine's face fell. "That's a good reason as any for drinking that much."

Chapter 4

The Blue-Wing cafe had a small, shining blue fairy on the sign and every single one of their cups. They gave out mugs if you were drinking in the cafe. Bianka wrapped her hands around the ceramic, trying to absorb caffeine and heat through her fingertips. Serenity was asleep with her favorite stuffed rabbit and a book to read when she woke up. She always stayed curled up in bed the day after an attack, but that didn't mean she couldn't read or play.

The local artist featured on the walls this week had done a series of portraits of chairs and vases. They made her twitch a bit when she stared at them. What possessed a person to paint chairs? Was it just that they didn't run away when asked to stay still? Or was it some sort of statement on grief? She shook her head in horror at her own thoughts. Blue better show up soon or she was out of this insanity creating place.

Blue settled across from her with some sort of drink with too much whipped cream and chocolate shavings on top served in a bowl-sized mug. "Thank you for joining me." Her dark glasses still covered her eyes and made it seem that she was hiding bruising or something else. She hesitated before removing them. Her eyes were the grey of summer rain clouds. She'd ringed them with blue glitter and tiny stones that were glued – no they were piercings that ran along her eyebrows. The bug glasses lay on the table between them a silent connection.

"I lost my first child when she was three," Blue stated. "She was bitten by a spider and reacted badly to the venom." Her voice was icy. She sipped her coffee concoction. "My second died when he was ten. He was killed by a stray bullet. My third was taken away by her father to live in his country. I didn't fight. Not then. I wasn't in any position to do so." She met Bianka's eyes with a fierce gaze.

Bianka cocked her head to the side. "Serenity's father slipped away in the middle of the night when she was in the hospital. He left me a present of jewelry that wouldn't kill her when I passed it on and just enough cash to get us through until I could start working again. I had to push that though, and she was still in the hospital when I started working again."

"What a beautiful name," Blue said.

"Thank you. Speaking of names, I'm Bianka McAllister."

Blue hesitated. "Most people call me Peri. Peri Jones." She offered her hand awkwardly.

Bianka shook it. Peri was one of those women who held her hand as though you were supposed to kiss it. She considered doing just that to see how she'd respond, but it wasn't worth the risk. Blue needed someone to listen to her. And if she could help someone the way Jasmine had helped her, then it was worth any sort of awkwardness. "Nice to meet you, Peri."

Blue smiled at that. It made her face light up. There were small lines in the corners of her eyes. They were probably around the same age. "It's been a long time since I heard that and it wasn't sarcastic. A pleasure to meet you Bianka McAllister."

A quiet sort of reverence rounded out the sound of her name and Bianka blinked at it a bit. She heard something like the chime of a church bell surround her for a moment. The touch of children's laughter followed it. She blinked back tears. "Thank you." There was a lull then as they both stared into their drinks.

Blue took a deep breath. "I am not normally hesitant like this. I've gotten used to having my own way and I've forgotten how to talk to someone I don't want to boss around. I'm going to try to get my child back from my husband." She lifted her eyes. "To do so, I need to take a shopping trip to a very specialized market. A rather dangerous market, truth be told. I'm not a fighter, Bianka."

"Do you want me to teach you to throw idiots?" Bianka studied Blue's delicate build. She wouldn't have the physical strength to do half the things Bianka did. She could use the little bit of Krav Maga Bianka'd taken as a teenager, but not the boxing.

"I'd like you to go with me."

Bianka froze. "Where?"

"It's called The Black Market. Anything you want is for sale there." Blue leaned forward, delicate fingers resting on Bianka's wrist. "Anything. Things to heal, things to kill, people to fight for you, information."

Bianka snorted. "Nice story. Where are we really supposed to go? Chinatown?"

Blue's eyes narrowed. She lifted her hand and the room around them seemed to freeze in place. A shine of blue glitter covered all of them. "I'm telling the truth. Do you believe in magic, Bianka McAllister?"

"I don't believe in anything," she replied.

Blue laughed at that. "Not even what you see with your own eyes. Go ahead, reach out, touch them. Steal their wallets. Do whatever you like. They won't stir. We're out of time now."

"If that's true, why do you need me to go with you? You can simply freeze anyone who's going to attack."

She looked at the closest man. "I cannot move from my position. I can only do this magic for someone else. I could freeze time. You could remove the threat, but I cannot do it by myself."

"That's not useful." Bianka stood carefully and investigated the room. She peered out the front door. The street was frozen. It seemed the world was on pause. She looked at her cheap digital, pink, princess watch. She'd picked it up at a discount store because it didn't have any exposed metal on it. She didn't dare let Serenity wear it. She wasn't sure that the back was actually completely plastic. The time seconds didn't count down as she looked. She sat down. She didn't feel any different. She hadn't let go of her coffee until after this little incident, so it wasn't a drug. Unless there was some new skin absorbed hallucinogen that she'd been dosed with when they shook hands.

"All magic has a price." Blue looked listless. "I used it to save my children until the day I wasn't able to do so. I couldn't stop the poison from taking Lily from me. I couldn't stop the bullet from hitting Pawpaw." She looked up. "What would you pay to cure your daughter?"

"Anything." That was the truth. Even if she had to die to make it happen.

"Then come with me. It will be no more than a week. I will make up for lost wages."

Bianka considered. A week away from Serenity. Would her mother go for it? She couldn't take Serenity into some place she didn't know. How could she protect her from something unpredictable?

"Your daughter could accompany us."

"She has contact allergies."

Blue looked at her for a long moment. "To what?"

"Metals. Everything except silver or platinum. Even pure gold sets her off."

The other woman startled. "That is a rare allergy indeed here. Not so rare in The Market."

Bianka could hear the capitals. "I will not risk my daughter's life."

"Even if the cure is found there?"

"Once I've found it, I can bring it home or bring her there. I'm not taking her."

Blue nodded calmly. "Very well." With a wave, the sound of multiple people talking, the grinder growling, and the barista calling people's names flooded back and around them like a tidal wave. "Will you come with me?"

"I have to make arrangements. And you have to tell me exactly what you want, first."

"I want you to protect me."

"Let me talk to my mother. What's the best way to reach you?"

"I'll meet you at the bar in two days. Be prepared for a week's journey, with little in the way of electrical accessibility or phones."

"What about food?"

"Allow me to take care of that."

Bianka nodded. "I need to get home." If it was a drug, it should wear off long before they met again. "And if you need to stop drinking? I can help you with that."

Blue startled. "Wine barely affects me. I'll be fine."

"Right because polishing off five hundred dollars of wine in a night isn't an issue?"

"Exactly." The other woman slid on her sunglasses. "I will see you in two days, Bianka McAllister."

Chapter 5

Serenity worked through the math workbook with a deep frown. She was using a mechanical pencil because she didn't have to use a pencil sharpener with it. Her fingers were awkward on the small body of the pencil. She'd never used any other type of pencil though, so she didn't know that her delicacy was strange in a child her age. She finished the sheet with a sigh. "I'm done. Can I go back to reading now?" Her hair was pulled up into a puff with actual ribbons which always startled the social workers and teachers that came by on a regular basis.

"Have you even looked at your science book today?"

"Don't feel like it. My head's still fuzzy." Serenity pouted and rubbed at her eyes. She never rubbed at her eyes if she was actually fuzzy. She just sort of drifted like she'd been smoking something she shouldn't.

Bianka's eyes narrowed. "That might work on Miss Elsa, but I'm wise to you." Miss Elsa was the teacher that came by the house every few days to make sure her daughter was actually learning and bringing county approved teaching materials.

Serenity sighed. "Fine. I'll do the science. It's just so boring."

"Why is it boring?"

"I know all of that stuff. Anyone with eyes knows where their stomach is. And they use stupid names like tummy. I'm not a kid."

"Hate to break it to you, but you really are." Bianka thought for a moment. "Let's do the tests for the end of the year and then we can focus on the stuff you don't know. And if you pass it, then we'll ask the proctor to come over and let you test out to second grade science, okay?"

"Cool!" Serenity hugged her tightly. Bianka rested her cheek on her head.

"What would you do if Mommy had to go away for a week?"

"A whole week?" Serenity's eyes were wide. "Why?"

"There's someone who insists they can fix your allergies. I don't trust them yet, so I want to talk to them before I take you anywhere. If this turns out to be some exposure-based cure, I'll shove it down their throats and come home. If it's something safer? I want to talk to Dr. Marx about it first."

Her daughter was very still. "So, I'd be able to actually wear earrings like Cynthia?" Cynthia was Serenity's best friend. She suffered from a severely compromised immune system. Serenity visited her once a week through the isolation walls of her room. The fact that Cynthia could wear earrings when Serenity couldn't was a matter of great fascination and discussion between the girls. Cynthia was not expected to live into adulthood. Neither was Serenity.

"I don't know. It depends on if this is just some scam to steal our money or if it's real."

Her daughter considered that for a long moment. "Would I stay with Nana? What about testing into a new class?"

"I can give you the test today and we can set up a study schedule. I can ask Miss Elsa to come work through the schedule with you. When I get back after that, we can do the formal testing."

"Okay." She curled up on her mother's lap though.

"What's wrong?"

"Will you go away forever like Dad did?"

She should have anticipated that. It was the first time she'd even considered leaving for longer than a day. An overnight with Nana was a lot different than Mommy being away for a week. "No. I promise. I will come back." Blue's voice echoed in her head 'what price would you pay?'.

"Will it hurt?"

"What do you mean?"

"They tried to do a blood marrow transplant for Cynthia. She said it hurt a lot. And that time they had to cut my throat hurt a lot."

Bianka held her more tightly. She had run directly into the emergency room screaming, she can't breathe at the nurse. Dr. Marx had figured out the metal allergy shortly after that. There'd been a panicked sort of Craigslist free-for-all to get rid of all of the metal she could. Plastic utensils and wooden furniture that she'd traded for with the other residents of the building. Jewelry had gone to the pawn shop; faucets were covered with plastic or electrical tape. The flat iron for her hair had gone to her mother. And her sister had taken all the bobby pins and helped sort through all the makeup in the medicine cabinet.

"I don't know, sweetheart. I'll make sure to ask a lot of questions and we'll discuss it when I get home. That's all assuming Nana can take care of you for the week." Serenity's head moved against her neck in a nod.

"What if it costs a lot of money?"

"We'll figure out a way to pay. That is not your problem." Bianka cursed the fact that so much of her money went to rent and medical bills that Serenity couldn't have half the things she wanted. She hated the fact that, 'we can't afford that' was something she had to say on a regular basis. It had gotten better as she'd grown up, but still. "Okay. Science test. Get your thinking cap on and I'll go get the paperwork."

Serenity slipped off of her lap. She straightened up the vintage fifties' coffee table. Bianka had done her homework on it when she was a kid and seeing her daughter working there always made her a little homesick. Maybe it was time to bend and take Mom's offer and move back home. If only she could convince her mother to come live with her instead.

Chapter 6

"How was your date?" Jasmine asked as she put up the last of the chairs.

"It was not a date."

"Good looking girl with similar style choices asks you out for coffee and you spend the next two days thinking about her and bring clothes for an overnight stay. Sounds like a date."

"I did not spend two days thinking about her. She offered me a one-week job. She's going up against her ex-husband and she's scared."

"So, you're going to be her bodyguard?"

"I'm considering it. Only if you can take my hours though. I hate to do that to you, but"

"Stop it. I'm taking your hours and happily enough. Chester will spell me. And we all know that Jumbo Jim doesn't give a damn who does the tending, just that it gets done. You can give me a bonus or something. You know, like those baked goods your mother makes. The ones with all the nuts in them?"

"Oh, the Persian nut square things? I'm still trying to figure out where she got that recipe. Sure."

Jasmine leaned against the doors. "You will be contacting us though. Just to let us know that you're alive and not rotting away in some drug den."

"She says it's sort of country, so I don't know what sort of coverage there is."

Jasmine nodded, accepting that. "Custody battles, ug. Sometimes I think the legal system in the country is just whacked." She gave Bianka a hug. "Please be careful. I know you're used to taking hits, but it worries me."

Bianka hugged back. Jasmine, despite her name, smelled more like vanilla and sandalwood. "You be careful too. Don't let the idiots push you around. And call for backup if you need it. I know that Emilio is more than willing to work as a bouncer if you need him."

"And what's your plan if she pushes you to drink with her?" Jasmine made sure they were making eye contact. It was an old habit that served them well.

Bianka lifted her head. "Tell her that I don't drink. Then, walk away if she won't stop."

"And if you're in a bad situation and worried about her safety?"

"Tell her that drinking means I can't protect her."

"And if there's pretty little pills on offer?"

Bianka paused. "I hadn't thought about that. I've seen her eyes without the shades. She wasn't high then, but that doesn't mean she doesn't use. Tell her that I don't take pills. Thank her and move on."

Jasmine nodded slowly. "And if there's a craving? Or your surrounded by people like your old crew?"

"Look at Serenity's picture."

"Good. When is she meeting you?"

There was a knock on the door and they both laughed. "I think she's here." Bianka looked through the one-way glass next to the door. She opened the door. "Hello, Blue."

Blue raised her brows. "Peri. Please."

"Peri then." There was no reason she couldn't keep thinking of her as Blue anyway. "Jasmine, this is Peri. Peri, Jasmine."

They shook hands. Jasmine studied Peri critically. "If you ever want help to stop drinking, drop by and ask. I've been sober for fifteen years now."

Peri pushed her glasses to the top of her head. The grey eyes studied Jasmine for a long moment. "Thank you for the offer. My drinking is under control."

Jasmine nodded. "Take good care of Bee here. Make sure she calls at least once every other day or so, okay? We worry. You have your charger and the extra batteries?"

"Yes, Jazz." They hugged again, then Jasmine faded out toward the back room. Bianka picked up her duffle bag from behind the counter. Blue's brows rose. "When are we leaving?"

"Right now."

"Where's your bag?"

To Market

"In the car." Blue gestured to the side. There was a powder blue Honda by the curb. There was a unicorn sticker on the back trunk and a vinyl fairy on the back window. Bianka tossed her bag in the backseat. Her black cargo pants and tank top under flannel made her feel underdressed. Black monochrome was much easier for traveling though. She'd gotten in the habit when she was practically living in the hospital. Blue settled her layered skirt into place around her in the front seat. Her rings sparkled in the rising sun as they set off.

"Where are we heading exactly?"

Blue grinned at her. "It'll be a surprise. Just trust me." The early morning traffic was light enough to let them get under way with minimal trouble. About an hour later they were out of the city and on their way to somewhere. Electronica filled the silence and Bianka let it wipe the worries out of her head for now. She leaned back and watched the scenery pass them by. The suburbs rolled away. They stopped at a gas station for coffee and fuel. "Why don't you catch a nap? I'll wake you up in an hour."

"But I have this wonderful coffee to keep me awake." The road tar in her cup would keep her awake. It would kill her stomach lining too.

Blue laughed at that, a peal of bells from a horse's harness in Central Park. "Please. Don't torture yourself. Sleep. It's safe as houses."

Bianka closed her eyes for just a moment. Blue poked her in the side. "It's been an hour," she said over the Swedish death metal on the radio. "And you should be awake for this part." She gunned the engine and drove directly at the graffiti filled wall. Bianka wished - not for the first time - that she was a screamer.

Chapter 7

The wall shimmered as they went through it and dumped them into an overly saturated nightmare of colors. Bianka's senses were out of control. She swallowed hard and closed her eyes against the world of color. The screaming music managed to block out the majority of the outside noise. The engine stopped. She pried open one lid. Everything was so bright. It was as though they'd fallen into one of the Indian pictures that her yoga instructor in had pinned up to every available surface. She'd been tutoring him in Biology in exchange for the lessons.

Her stomach wanted to rebel, but she forced it to behave with practice earned through years of hangovers. "I'm glad I didn't drink that coffee," she mentioned.

Blue's laughter pealed again, clashing with the music. She turned off the radio. "I have an extra pair of sunglasses in the glove box."

"Thank Ford," she muttered. She pulled out the large glasses and put them on. The world dimmed immediately. She sighed in relief. "I can't get used to it this way though, but my stomach and brain thank you."

Blue patted her on the arm. "Our hotel is here. The Market is about a mile away." She pointed in the direction of the sunset. "I don't want to stay in The Market proper." Her nose wrinkled. "They have bad wine."

"I'm understanding why you drink." Bianka followed her with her duffle over her shoulder and Blue's bag in her hand.

"You don't have to carry that."

"It's heavy enough to use as a weapon. We're going to have a long talk before we go anywhere."

Blue hesitated. "Over dinner?"

"Is it actually safe for me to eat here? Every story I've ever heard says that's a bad idea. I'm beginning to think that's because it's all drugged."

"No, nothing like that." Blue walked through the lobby, which was a yellow that hurt the eyes to the desk which was fire-engine red. The clerk offered her a large gold key with a blue stone in it.

"If you'll sign the register, Miss Peri." The clerk's voice echoed in the room, like a badly auto-tuned song. That had better not be normal around here. The off-pitch melding would give her a headache. The room turned out to be suite – a ridiculously sized suite with two bedrooms, and a shared main room with its own small kitchen that had a stove and a coffee maker. The food in the cupboard appeared to be sealed and brand name. That was a step in the right direction. It should be safe and uncontaminated. She grimaced.

Blue had settled into her room, unpacking and showering everything with blue glitter. Bianka grimaced. She would have to wash everything twice at the laundromat, including her bag, just to eliminate as much of that as possible. Metal that could be inhaled. Swollen lungs, nose and throat. Fuck that noise. "Do not get the glitter all over me. Blue glitter is not intimidating."

Blue stuck her tongue out at her. "Right. No glitter on the boring bodyguard."

"Is that my official title? I could add it to my tee-shirt."

The other woman rolled her eyes. "Okay. So, you wanted to have a talk. Pour me some of that wine and we'll talk. And I won't get glitter all over you. Just on certain parts of you."

"Is Jasmine right? Is this actually a date?"

Laughter again. She might have to kill her employer. "No. I really need you for your ability to hammer-lock men who take a swing at me."

"Will you be provoking them? Or just being yourself because it could go either way?" Bianka handed over a glass of wine and settled in the armchair across from the chaise that Blue had chosen to sprawl over. She pushed the sunglasses to the top of her head. The colors were less painful in here. Mostly they were glowing aquas and blues. To match Blue's taste, she supposed.

"I have enemies because I don't live here. I live Out There. And In Here is so much different."

"And the father of your child lives where?"

"In Here," Blue admitted. "And it's his choice. I can't make it for him, obviously, but I want my child back and I can only do that here."

"So, this is a custody battle or are you planning to kidnap your kid?" Bianka wasn't sure which way to turn on that issue. It would depend on what the kid wanted.

"I need to get something before I confront him, you see, and that means I have to go to The Market. The Market isn't... that is to say, it's different than this part of town."

"Right. So we're going to Anacostia to pick up some illegal guns and you need muscle."

Blue grinned. "Close enough. You're still willing right?"

"I am." She rubbed her temple. "I need to adjust to this and you need to answer some questions. Okay?"

"Okay. As much as I can. I don't know everything."

"How much of this color saturation is you slipping me LSD on the trip?"

Glitter flew as Blue sat up. "None of it. This is real. I swear, this is real." She put a hand out, but didn't touch. She grimaced. "The father of your child never showed you any of this."

"How could he?"

"Your daughter is allergic to metal. That only happens with children who are half-fae. He was allergic to iron."

"Yes." Tension filled Bianka's stomach and tightened her shoulders. Nate had been gone for six years. He hadn't even stayed to see if Serenity survived. Fuck him. He was never getting near them again. He would never have the chance to hurt either of them. And if she ran into him here, she'd have to throw him out of a window or something.

"It's a lot to take in. But he should have shown you. He should have explained when he found out she had the allergies. What name did he use?"

"Nate Jones."

"Nate." Blue considered for a long moment. "I'll have to think about that one. It's easier. I'm Peri Here and There, but a Nate is probably something else here. Nasturtium or something. Pomegranate. What color was his hair?"

"He kept it dyed black. I never noticed his roots."

"Well that's no help. Darn."

"You're sure there's a cure for the allergy?"

"I'm positive. Everything is for sale at The Market. Everything." Blue grimaced. "But the cost is variable. It will depend on what you have to offer. Maybe it's lessons on Out There. Maybe it's the blood of an enemy."

"My enemy or theirs? At the moment I'd happily offer Nate's head."

"Careful now. You don't know what he is here. He could be a prince."

"Don't know. Don't care. He abandoned his daughter to medicine that kept trying to kill her and never even told me that it was something common or known. Fuck him."

"Rather not. I have enough troubles."

"What sort of weapons are allowed around here? I'm not exactly a sword swinger, but I can't imagine I can get my hands on a gun. Will fists be enough?"

"They should be. And you can keep any weapons you win off of attackers. Sort of an unwritten rule of conquest."

"And will we actually be coming back to this hotel every night?"

"Hopefully? I don't know. We might end up spending the night negotiating with someone."

"Will my phone work?"

Blue grimaced. She finished off her wine. "It'll work if you're in the car, but not in the hotel or anywhere else. The car is sort of a signal booster. I keep my phone out there in case I get a message from my assistant."

"What do you do in the real world?"

"Venture capital. I'm a very good negotiator."

"And you sneeze glitter on them if they don't behave."

Blue smirked.

"More practically. Is it safe for me to eat here? I don't have allergies the way Serenity does, but I'm not built for this place."

"Legends aren't always true. Let's say, eat anything you recognize. Don't eat anything you don't. That includes street fare that looks like meat. Seriously, if you don't recognize it, like an apple or Slim Jims, don't eat it. Anything in the hotel is safe. I had it packed with food from Harris Teeter. I'd have chosen a Piggly

Wiggly, but we're not close any of those states." She sighed wistfully. "It's such a cute name. Piggly Wiggly. Piggle Wiggle."

"Stop. Please. So, it's safe for me to eat here. Drink the water?"

"Also, safe. And the sodas are from Out There if you recognize the brands. We even have Shasta."

"I'm beginning to think you've been stalking me."

Blue stood up. "I'm going to get more wine. You want some?"

"I don't drink."

"Oh, right. Like your girlfriend at the bar."

Bianka didn't correct that. Jazz wouldn't mind and it might keep her out of trouble. Blue poured a full glass of wine. It was about a third of the bottle. "Does wine affect you? Or is it like drinking a soda?"

"For me? Like drinking a coke or a really, really weak beer. Just calories." Blue seemed to debate. "I need a lot of sugar to feel right. Think of it as reverse diabetes. Wine works well. Scotch works well. Soda and juice work really well. But wine is easiest to get here so, there's that."

"Will the color saturation die down? Am I just not used to it or what?"

"I really don't know what you're talking about, so I'm going to guess it'll die down. You can use my sunglasses if you need them. I only ever really need them when I cross the border because the sun is always setting."

"So, it's always going to be washed in sunset colors?" Bianka cast a long look at the wine. One glass wouldn't hurt right? She closed her eyes and breathed through her nose. Natural high from controlled breathing should quell the need. If not? Well, she had Serenity's picture to look at as a reminder. She had to be strong for her.

Chapter 8

"Jazz, she drinks like a fucking fish and I totally empathize. This place is fucked-up." Bianka hung up as she finished her voicemail. She hoped the message actually went through. She put her car in the phone with Blue's. The walk to The Market was filled with birds in 1980's neon plumage and a giant preying mantis in the same color pink as Bianka's hair. The mantis gave her a stately bow. She returned the bow.

"Huh. He likes you," Blue said. "I didn't think he liked anyone."

"You don't have the right color hair. Punks have to stick together you know." No increased respiration, Bianka noted. I've never had a trip this intense or this long. She glanced down at her watch which was keeping proper time. Not a dream. Blue had her glasses on the top of her head, holding back her hair.

The Market's entrance turned out to be a huge black arch that rose at least three stories in the air. It was made of smooth marble. It was cold to the touch without any flecks of color or veining visible. Blue quivered a little bit while Bianka stroked the cold stone. The guard standing just inside had a sword longer than Bianka's arm. He raised his brows at them but didn't say anything.

"Tell me you aren't expecting me to fight something that has to duck to get through this."

"Of course not." Blue's eyes darted to the guard. "Well, only if you had help."

"Great. I'm comforted by that." Bianka stepped through the gate and nodded at the guard. Blue took her hand. Blue's hand was delicate, but her grip was tight and her fingers trembling. Bianka gave them a squeeze. Her eyes roamed over the crowd. It was Mardi Gras and a Greenwich Village Halloween after a few too many drinks and three tabs of acid.

"I need a drink," Blue muttered. She led the way past the first few stalls that were set up. Jewelry shimmered and glittered in a rainbow of colors. Silver like water cascaded over the sides of the booth. Chocolate from all over the world was laid out in neat rows on the other side. There was a crush of people around that booth. A harried looking woman in a bunny outfit was holding a tray of samples. One of her ears was crumpled and there was chocolate around her lips.

The place smelled like a rave that had been sprinkled with exotic spices. Incense wove through the street as they walked. A large man that looked more like a hippo than a human was serving sautéed cabbage and spinach from his booth. The steam rising up had made his sign run. Bianka couldn't read the prices or the actual names of his dishes. Blue's eyes were darting here and there, and she looked around the streets like a toddler pulling on the end of her leash. Bianka kept her grip steady. She saw an older woman selling woven belts. She paused at the booth.

"Are those wool or cotton?"

"Wool. From alpaca. Very soft, but strong. All handmade by women of my village."

Bianka studied the belts. They seemed normal enough. Blue came to rest next to her. "Oh, those are pretty," she said. "I like that one." It was a sea scene with little jumping fish on it.

"How much for this one?" Bianka pointed at the fish belt.

"For you? Ten dollars."

Bianka reached for the bag she kept around her neck. "No, no, I'll pay," Blue said. She handed over a twenty. The woman found a crumpled ten-dollar bill to hand back. She unhooked the belt and handed it over. Her lips quirked when Bianka tied one end around Blue's wrist and the other around her own.

"There, now we won't be separated."

The old woman laughed. It was a rusty sound that made the man in the next booth look over with surprise. Bianka winked at them both. Blue studied the belt that was now around her wrist. "Well, I guess," she said and then fluttered off to investigate the next thing that grabbed her attention. She wrapped her fingers around the knot on the belt as though to protect it. Bianka did the same. It wouldn't stop someone with a knife. Paranoia was such a wonderful thing.

There was music dribbling out from the more permanent storefronts. Bars, restaurants, and cafes she decided. Blue squealed in delight. "Oh, aren't they just adorable?" She held up a small, furry winged something. It had big black eyes and a pink furry body. "I think you need a pet."

"No, really, that's okay. I have enough trouble keeping myself and daughter alive. Another creature is a bad idea."

"Don't be silly. He takes care of himself."

"Thank you, but no."

"You are no fun. Oh, wine booth." She abandoned the furry whatever back into his box.

The pet dealer made a sour face at Blue's back. "Fairies," he snorted. He was tall and thin with skin like worn leather as though he'd been out in the sun for his entire life. He placed the little pink creature on her shoulder and it immediately curled up against her neck. He nodded once. "Tell him to run home if you get lost and he will bring you here."

"I couldn't."

"Make an old man happy. He matches your hair."

"Thank you."

Blue was drinking a large mug of warm spiced wine. "They have unfun cider too."

"I'm fine." The wine dealer's shop had large vats of spiced wine. Some of the customers had their own cups, then there were those like Blue who were borrowing pewter cups that looked as though they'd never been cleaned. The dealer had whiskers and moved like a mouse — fast and suspicious. "Where are we headed or are you just shopping?"

"He gave it to you! Hello, cutie." Blue stroked a finger down the pink-moth-hamster thing. "What his name?"

"He didn't say."

"Oh, he'll speak up soon enough, I'm sure."

Great, a talking fairy-hamster. "Again, are we headed somewhere in particular or are we just out for a walk?"

"I'll know it when I see it."

"No alcohol in the cider?" she asked the mouse-man. He studied her for a moment, then reached into a red cooler and pulled out a sealed ginger ale. "Oh, that's perfect." He handed it to her.

"One dollar." She paid him and took a deep gulp. She poured a little into the cover and held it for Pink-moth-hamster. Its little tongue flicked out to taste it, then to suck it down with a happy little purr. The ginger ale's familiar flavor refreshed her temper. She handed the empty bottle back to the mouse-man.

"You come back any time." His front teeth were large like a rodent's. "I always have ginger ale. Settles my stomach." He gestured at his customers with a roll of his eyes.

"I understand."

Blue handed back her empty cup. "Come on, there's a darling little shop just over." She paused. "Huh. I thought it was over there. Must have moved again." She left a little trail of blue glitter on the ground, but the only glitter on Bianka was on her hand where they'd actually touched. Blue had to have some sort of control over it. Now that she thought about it, there was glitter everywhere. Trails of blue, green, silver, bronze, purple, and everything in between filled the cracks between the cobblestones and the edges of the booths.

Blue tangled their fingers together, somewhat calmer now that she had another mug of wine in her. Bianka had no idea how the woman had stayed so still in the bar. Their wine wasn't that good. The Market was full of jewelry and handcrafted items mixed with food and drink stalls. Wait a minute, Bianka's head turned to stare at the booth full of guns. They were hanging from side of the booth. The dealer in the middle was a thin, androgynous figure in a blue jacket.

"Did you want a gun? I mean to feel safer?" Blue bit her lip.

"No, I just wasn't expecting them to be displayed like that."

Blue smiled. "When I said everything, I meant everything. Oh, don't step on the black tiles here. They set off traps." She pointed at the ground.

"What sort of traps?"

"Pranks mostly. Some sort of transformation into frogs or rabbits. That sort of thing. Some of them are deadly, but you can never be sure which ones are which."

Bianka managed a weak smile. "Wonderful."

Blue pulled her toward a booth with calmly swimming ducklings. "It's a duck pull. I haven't seen one of these since my Lily was little."

"Shouldn't those be rubber ducks?"

"Hush. It doesn't hurt them one bit." She offered the carnie a dollar and scooped up one of the little ducklings. "Isn't she cute? Red band on her ankle."

The carnie gave them a snagged-toothed smile and offered a tray of petit fours. Blue took one of the pink sugar topped ones. She put the duck back into the poor. "Cute." The carnie held the tray out for her. "No, thank you."

"Cute pet."

She patted the Pink-moth-hamster. "Yes, he is."

Carnie chuckled. "I was thinking about the other one. Fairy on a leash. Good job."

"Hey now!" Blue protested. "It's human on a leash, thank you very much." She sniffed theatrically.

"Didn't you have some shop you wanted to find?"

"Right. Thanks." Blue popped the other half of her treat into her mouth. She pulled Bianka behind her as they made their way through the press of people.

"FSM, is that a dick on a stick?"

"Anything you want. I wouldn't recommend buying one though. The barbecue sauce the crones use is nasty."

"I am not asking how you know that." Blue pulled her into a bookstore that was a lurid shade of orange. "Dutch fan?"

"How did you guess, my dear?" There was an old woman behind the desk. Her hair was up in a simple bun and her glasses had a chain decorated with orange baubles. Her suit was orange and white. There was an orange butterfly perched in her hair. "What can I find for you?"

"I'm just here to carry bags," Bianka protested. "Although, if you have anything on metal allergies, I'd appreciate taking a look at it."

"And you little Miss Peri?"

"Just point me at the law section."

"Three shelves that way. I'll find you there?"

Bianka held up their linked wrists. "Yes, ma'am."

Blue selected a stack of books and settled down at the table in the center of the shelves. The owner returned with four books. "This is all I have at the moment. I keep asking for more science books, but they just don't ever turn up."

"Thank you." Bianka accepted them and settled down next to Blue. So, You're Raising a Changeling, Do You Really Love that

Human, and two versions of How to Avoid Iron Poisoning. She set aside the iron poisoning books and flipped open the indexes on the other two. Changelings, she discovered were actually fae children that were raised as humans. That didn't help her. The last book, however, made her want to strangle Nate. Metal allergies were a known syndrome in "mixed-species" children. "Fatal in 75% of cases. Most children don't make it to adulthood," she murmured. "Fuck that. Serenity's going to be the 25%."

The owner settled across from them. "You have a fae child?" she asked. "My daughter is considering the option right now."

"It turns out her father was fae," Bianka allowed. "I just knew he had an iron allergy."

"I'm Tulip. Your daughter developed the metal allergy?"

"Yes."

"Which means she also has magic. Or will if she survives long enough. My daughter thinks she's in love with the man she's dating."

"Does he know?"

Tulip looked away. "I don't know."

"He needs to know if they're planning on children. Illness can tear families apart faster than lies."

"I'll point that out to her. Has your daughter shown signs of magic yet?"

"No."

"Chapter seven in that book is very good at explaining the types of magic that mixed-species children develop."

"Thank you, Tulip."

"I'll be at the front desk if you need anything." The owner left them.

"The cure won't be in a book," Blue said.

"But at least I know I'm not alone in this. You don't know how much of a difference just knowing that makes." She turned her attention to her book. Her fingers shook as she made it through the first chapter. "Do all of you think like this? That humans are too stupid to understand your culture?"

Blue shifted uncomfortably. "Not stupid, exactly, just not capable of understanding all the nuances."

"Because you've kept us in the dark for how many years? Manipulating those you did let in. And did you forget to mention something about how time works here?"

The fae woman cleared her throat. "The Market isn't like proper Underhill. It's a one to one here. One minute Here is one minute There."

"And you weren't going to take me into Underhill?"

"No."

"And your little freeze trick. Does that actually work here?"

"Yes, of course."

"How long before you told me that all half-fae children die before they turn twenty?"

"There's a cure. I know there is."

"Have you seen it?"

"I researched it when I considered marrying a human man. I've found references to it at least ten times."

"Where?"

"The Black Market. Right outside those doors. You just have to be willing to look for it."

"Where are your sources?"

"They're in Underhill. But they're real. I swear on my wine."

Tulip returned with a pot of tea and two cups. "Would you like some paper to take notes?"

"No thank you."

The Pink-moth-hamster rubbed his head against Bianka's throat. She poured a bit of the tea into her saucer for him but didn't drink any herself. Tulip frowned at her. Bianka smiled as sweetly as she could manage and went back to the details of courting in the fae world compared to the human world. Nate had courted her according to the rules in this book. She could see that clearly. He'd just never asked her to marry him. Bastard.

The next page listed the magic that Serenity could develop. She blanched. A child prodigy was considered magic. So, she was showing signs of magic. Then again, if being a prodigy counted as magic, so had Bianka. It was why she'd started partying. It stopped her brain and let her be normal for once.

Chapter 9

"Please tell me you're joking. We're going to shop with a dragon?"

"No, no, we're going shopping for a dragon. That way, when we give him his gift, he'll want to help us out." Blue acted as though that made perfect sense.

"And this is what you found in your book yesterday?" Blue nodded. Bianka rubbed her eyes. She wanted more sleep. Pink-moth-hamster settled on her shoulder and bumped her face. She petted it gently on the head. "I need a name to call you," she informed it. "Okay, so what are we shopping for exactly? Gold, jewelry? Sudoku books?"

"He'd probably enjoy a puzzle book." Blue tapped her teeth. It was a nervous habit that she'd never displayed before. "But I was thinking more polish for his scales."

"And where in The Market do we find that? Do you have any idea, or do we just start asking dealers as we get through the door and go until we're lost again?"

"We weren't lost yesterday, just temporarily not where we were supposed to be."

"Lost."

"Spoilsport. We should be able to get the polish at the someplace that sells swords. It's the same sort of thing." She waved a hand in the air. "And then we'll just need to find the dragon."

"Oh, Find the dragon. Sure. That's easy. We'll just look for the cave with the empty armor in front of it."

Blue giggled. "They don't actually eat knights."

"They're not vegetarians."

"No, but they're happy enough with sheep and that sort of thing. Humans don't have a lot of meat on them really."

"Right." Bianka sipped her coffee. Instant oatmeal and coffee and a cherry lollipop for when she was done with the good-for-her shit. "Is there jerky in the kitchen?"

"I'll check. Are you going to use the belt today? Should I get you a collar?"

"No, I just like having my hands free on occasion. To feel pink-moth-hamster here."

"Pink-moth-hamster is not a good name."

"Pinkachu."

"Gesundheit."

"Exactly my problem. I don't know what to call it."

"He'll let you know. Just listen to him."

"Are you sure it's a he?"

Blue returned with a packet of beef jerky. Bianka put it into the lower pocket of her cargo pants. "Pretty sure. I didn't really look, but he feels like a he."

"Pink-moth-hamster it is for now then."

The Market wasn't as overwhelming this time. Bianka had resigned herself to the noise and color. The strange reverb issues had resolved themselves. Everyone's voices sounded normal. But she was still hearing colors when she looked too long at patterned fabrics. She just had to ride the trip out now. Serenity's voice on the phone had helped ground her this morning.

The sword dealer was deeper into The Market than Blue had thought. There was a crone selling apples and ribbons and every hair on the back of Bianka's throat stood up. "So, how true are the fairy tales I learned growing up?"

"Depends on where you learned them."

"Like poisoned apples and ribbons that choke the life out of you?"

"Oh, those are mostly true." Blue looked over at the apple vendor. "She's mostly harmless if you wanted to get some ribbons for Serenity's hair. Just tell them they're for your little girl."

"That's okay. We have enough trouble deciding on colors in the morning. Getting one of those variegated ones would just send us over the edge." She hadn't brought much cash and she really didn't want to think about what else she might trade. She'd almost started selling drugs once, just to finance the alcohol habit, but she hadn't. This place made her think about it. Everything was legal and nothing seemed regulated. Not even weapons.

"And this is a nice knife. Be a good one to give your pet," the sword dealer said to Blue.

Blue rolled her eyes. "I'm looking for scale polish. I've got dragon scale at home and it's looking dingy."

"Not enough sparkle for you, eh?" The dealer stroked his matinee villain mustache. "I've got regular polish and polish with built in glitter. It'll change to any color you ask for."

Blue studied both bottles. "Does the glitter work on all types of dragon scale or just faux dragon? I thought regular was too hard for glitter polish?"

"Well, it's better on faux," he admitted. "And if it's old-school real dragon? You'll actually want this polish. It'll take off years of neglect if it's used properly."

Bianka tuned out the discussion of dragon polishing to study the knife he'd been showing off. It was an all black knife with a sturdy handle wrapped in leather. It fit her hand well. The blade had no hook or bends. It had good balance. Jasmine had gotten her into knife throwing as a way to distract her from cravings. It might be good to take it up while she was here. Half the people in the streets were carrying some sort of weapon. She flipped the knife experimentally. There was a target set up in the booth. "Do you mind?" she asked the dealer gesturing at it. He shook his head with a smirk. Men. She threw the knife and it embedded itself well in the wood. He stared at it and then back at her. He turned to Blue.

"So, you don't want her armed? Because that was frightening and very attractive at the same time."

"Shut up, Lyco." A woman poked her head out from behind the curtain at the back of the booth. "Did you just let someone throw knives at me without warning again?"

"Cheaper than a divorce," he muttered. "No dear!"

She looked at the knife. "Throw it at his head next time," she yelled at Bianka, then ducked away again.

Bianka turned her best "stop being an idiot before I throw you out the door" glare. Lyco smiled at her, showing too many teeth. "So, do you have anything similar to that one? It's got good balance, but it's a bit too heavy."

"Know what? Kill my wife and I'll give you anything in the shop."

"I heard that!" the sharp voice from the back room yelled.

"Good!" He shrugged. "I've got some knives that are actually for throwing, but they're too small for your hands." He fetched the knife from the target. "So, what do you say, glitter or no?"

"No glitter. I'll take the young dragon polish though. I don't think my scale is close to a thousand yet. And that knife for Bee." Blue smiled at him. "Unless you saw something you like better?"

"No, the others here are all for show."

Lyco scowled at both of them. "No sense of showmanship. It's sad how this younger generation has forgotten how to look good." He shoved a sheath at her. "You'll want that so you can clip it onto your hip. Looks are important. There's a leather shop about three blocks that way."

Blue paid for their purchases. Bianka put the knife on her hip. It felt as though it should have always been there. She looked up, but the shop was empty. No merchandise. No dealer. Not even the fabric remained. Blue shrugged. "These things happen."

Fuck, this was the longest flashback she'd ever had. It had to be. "Off to the next stop then."

"Wait a minute, dearie," the apple vendor said.

"Ma'am?" Blue asked.

"Not you." She turned to Bianka. "You'll want this." She held up a black ribbon.

"I'm afraid I don't have anything to trade for it."

The old woman shook her head. "It's a gift." Her teeth were surprisingly white and even when she smiled. "You've tamed a fairy after all." She coiled up the black ribbon and pressed it into Bianka's hand. "Use it well."

"Thank you." The old woman patted her arm. She smelled like apple pie up close. Bianka put the ribbon into her pocket.

"You haven't tamed me," Blue stated. "I tamed you."

"Sure."

Blue stuck out her tongue. She tugged on the belt a bit. "This way. Down the alley. It's a cut through."

"Oh, this is a wonderful idea." She caught Blue's fingers in her own. "In my experience alleys are where you go when you're about to be killed."

"It's perfectly safe." Blue pulled her into the alley. Colors steamed by them. Images of snakes and blood and spiders crawled up the colored walls. Pressure pressed down on Bianka's chest until it was hard to breathe. She tightened her grip on Blue's fingers and fought down vertigo and nausea. There were bad things hiding in the colors and every nerve of her body knew it. She wanted to close her eyes but couldn't. She had to be on guard. The bad things were coming for them.

They exited the colors on the other side of The Market. Bianka swallowed hard. Pink-moth-hamster chittered angrily at both of them, then crawled down her shirt to settle in her cleavage. It shivered and she petted its head in comfort. "That was fun."

Blue looked at her with a frown. "You saw something that I didn't see? It's just an alley that cuts between one side and the other."

"You don't get the rush of colors, bad trip imagery, and the feeling that you're about to die?"

"No, I see cobblestones and brick walls with a lot of trash on the side."

"You're going to get me killed. I just know it."

"Don't be silly. You won't die in an alley. You'll die in glorious battle with the giant over there that's looking at us."

Bianka glanced over at the so-called giant. He was, actually, a giant. He stood a good twelve feet tall with broad shoulders and a bag over his shoulder. There was flour up and down his front. He was looking at the two of them with the sort of smile that her uncle had when confronted with small children playing with puppies. She waved at him and he lifted a hand in response. "He's fine. Now which way?"

Blue stared at her. "You waved at a giant?"

"I waved at a twelve-foot-tall baker."

"Seriously. You waved at a giant and he didn't immediately try to eat you. Are you sure you're human?"

"One hundred percent."

"Okay." Blue's eyes narrowed, looking more like a thunderstorm than a sun shower at the moment. "This way." She turned in a spray of glitter that covered Bianka's pants from knee to ankle. That was never going to come out.

Chapter 10

The dragon's lair was not a cave. It was not a mansion. It was a row house of brown brick with filigreed iron bars on the windows and carved marble surrounds with runes and Cyrillic and English all jumbled together into twisting vines. Blue hesitated at the door. The knocker was a large horseshoe. "You knock."

"You actually have an iron allergy, don't you?"

"Maybe? Sometimes. Yes."

"Right." Bianka lifted the knocker and rapped three times. The door opened to reveal a small man with a perfectly pressed black suit.

"May I help you?"

Blue cleared her throat. "I'm here to see Andre Draconis please."

The man studied them both. His eyes lingered on the knife and the belt that connected their wrists. Bianka stood straight under the regard, but Blue fidgeted with her hair. She dragged her glasses down over her eyes. She picked at the knot at her wrist. The man inclined his head. "Enter." He stepped aside to let them cross the threshold, then closed and locked the door behind them. He led them to a parlor. "Please sit down. I will talk to the master."

The door of the parlor shut. The parlor was done in soft creams and raspberry. Ornate Victorian needlework covered the chairs and shades dripping with jade beads covered each of the sconces. The light was soft, indirect and left shifting shadows and strange glittering colors on the walls and furniture. Heavily carved wood frames were upholstered with cream velvet. Blue perched on one of the chairs. Bianka settled on the loveseat that was near it. "Should we untie this?"

Blue's fingers stopped worrying the knot. "No, I don't want to be separated. And who knows what sort of magic there is here." She looked up. "You think of it as a toddler leash, and mother's protection is part of it now."

Bianka blushed. "I do. But if it's embarrassing to you."

"Never that. No. It means you care, no matter how many people think it's something else. It's safer this way. For both of us."

Bianka didn't know what to say, so she just nodded. She sat up straight. "Will this glitter get onto his rugs?" She pointed at her legs.

"No. The rugs have some sort of anti-dirt protection on them."

"Scotch guard," a voice from the doorway said. "Thank you for your worry, Miss?"

"Bee. And this is Blue." If the old stories were true, giving away your real name was just begging for trouble.

Blue glanced at her but didn't correct anything. Draconis was a tall, thin man with angular, sharp features. His nose was long, like a raptor's beak made human. His lips were thin, and his skin had a slightly purple tint to it. His hair was black as were his eyes. They were completely black like the Pink-moth-hamster that sat in Bianka's cleavage and ignored them all. Bianka stood to shake hands with him, but he didn't offer his hand, simply nodded to both of them and settled in the overstuffed armchair by the fireplace. Bianka settled back down next to Blue.

"And what brings you to my humble home?" His voice was soft and faintly amused. He looked at Bianka expectantly.

Blue cleared her throat. "I came to ask for your assistance in a family matter, sir."

"Oh?" He raised his brows and steepled his fingers. Sweet, singing serpents, he was doing his best to be Sherlock Holmes. Bianka could only hope he was intelligent enough to carry it off. "You wish to marry a human?" he teased.

Blue rolled her eyes. "No, Bee is just looking after me. My ex-husband has been keeping me from seeing my child. I need to find him and to find a way to regain custody. I was told that you were the sharpest legal mind in The Market. Were they wrong?"

Draconis cocked his head to the side and studied them both. "You lost control of your child's fate through the flightiness that is standard in fairies of your breed. And now you wish to regain it why?"

"I now have the means and the place to give her a proper life."

"And if she will not leave Underhill? What will you do then?"

Blue trembled at the thought. "Then, I will visit. I will not have my child raised without me."

"Ah. And now your stubbornness appears. And what do you offer me in exchange for this information?"

"I have scale shine as a small token. Beyond that, I am open to negotiation."

"I rarely work for such amenable women. Linneas," he called. The butler appeared. Blue placed the scale shine bottle on the tray. "These women are currently my clients. They are allowed to approach at any time. Though, I do hope you'll not interrupt me late at night. A dragon needs his rest."

Bianka smiled at that.

"And for you, Bee?"

"I'm looking for the cure to my daughter's metal allergy. I was told it was somewhere in The Market."

He didn't speak for a long moment. "It is indeed. And what do you have to offer me?"

"Nothing. This is purely Blue's stop."

He leaned forward. "It needn't be. You have a child. As of yet unwed?"

"She's seven. Back down."

"A small vial of her blood, an innocent virgin's blood, would go far in The Market. I would wager that it's innocent, magical blood at that."

"I'll search on my own. Thank you." She filed the information away.

"When you change your mind, the offer stands. A vial of blood for the name of a Healer who can help you."

She nodded. "You and Blue have negotiating to do."

Draconis turned his attention away from her and that was a relief. She studied his profile as he talked. "And what do you offer?"

"Money. Gold and jewels if you prefer. Antiques from Out There."

"Your talent, Periwinkle, is time." Blue stiffened at the sound of her name. "Yes, I know exactly who you are. However, your supposition about the belt was correct. At the moment, magic considers you to be Bee's child and thus, the name I know for you is not correct." He crossed the room to stand over them. "I will assist you, Blue. For the cost of one favor of my choosing."

"I will not give up my child or my life to you."

"No, a favor of time. I will need to... reproduce soon and need time to do so properly. Agreed?"

"You help me get my daughter back and I will help you create your child. Agreed." He left them in the sitting room. Bianka looked around at the flickering shadows.

"I don't know what the etiquette is here. Do we stick around, or do we come back in a few hours?"

"He didn't tell us to leave and his bulter hasn't told us to leave, so we'll stay for the moment." Blue twitched. "I think he likes you."

"Likes me?"

"Yes, you didn't want anything from him. Not like me." Blue looked down. She picked at the edge of her nail. "I know I can't do this alone. And he's the best lawyer. He really is."

"Which is why you should have gotten your agreement in writing."

Blue startled at that. "No, no. I would never imply that his honor was broken."

"It's not honor, it's common sense. Lawyers know the law. They can find a loophole at any time. You didn't define help. And you didn't get a timeframe of when he'd need your help."

Laughter turned their heads to the door. Draconis leaned against the doorframe, bent over in laughter. He smiled at them, exposing sharp white teeth. He was a predator. An actual predator and Bianka judged whether they could make it past him while he was laughing. "I do like you, Bee. And I will answer your questions as they are reasonable ones. I will provide an address for where Periwinkle's husband is hiding. I will provide legal documents to allow her child to stay with her, so long as the child agrees. The husband's agreement is unnecessary. Periwinkle's fairy clan is matrilineal. You have no other daughters, correct?"

"Yes." Blue's voice was soft.

Draconis' face softened a bit. "I am sorry for what losses you've incurred. In exchange, Periwinkle will provide a space out of time for my... reproduction to occur."

"And your reproduction will not interfere with her raising her child?"

"Not in the least. Time will not have moved forward an inch during the time we are secluded. Periwinkle may need a few days' rest, but nothing more." He stepped forward. "As for you, Bee. I do like you. And I will tell you this without any need for bargains. The cure you seek is available, but it is dangerous, painful, and may only have partial success."

"Could it kill her?"

"You will have to talk to the healer about that. I'm afraid I cannot answer medical questions of that nature."

"You are a lawyer." Bianka frowned. "Does her father have any legal claim on her? He never married me, simply left me with a child and some silver."

"In cases such as these, Underhill judgements favor the mother. If he were to try for custody, they would ask why he didn't steal her away when he left you."

"Right. That's one good thing out of all of this then."

"You are welcome in my home and at my table any time, dear ladies. I'll have Linneas show you out." He bowed to them. "Tomorrow at this time to pick up your documents, Periwinkle."

Chapter 11

"Hi, Mom!" Serenity's voice was full of excitement. "So, what did you do yesterday?"

"I met a dragon," she told her. "And he says that the cure is real, but that it's going to be hard to deal with."

Her daughter laughed. "So, the dragon said that it would work?" She obviously believed she meant doctor. Oh, the poor kid had no idea.

"That it might work." Bianka had never lied to her daughter about medical procedures. "It might not work, but in either situation, it's going to hurt."

"Oh." The voice on the other end was subdued. "Hurt how?"

"All over. Remember when we talked about bone marrow transplants with Cynthia?"

"Yes. She said it hurt lots. And it didn't work. She still has to live in the same room." Serenity was quiet. "But the doctors never said anything about doing a transplant on me."

"I'm still trying to understand all the details. I'll explain it when I do, okay, sweetheart?"

"Yes, Mom. What else did you do?"

"I sat with someone who was trying to get her daughter back from her husband. The lawyer was pretty sure it wouldn't be an issue."

"The someone you want to help the way Aunt Jasmine helped you?"

"Yes."

"Okay." Serenity knew Jasmine's name, but none of the other people Bianka knew from rehab.

"What would you do if your father suddenly showed up and asked you to come with him?" Bianka slouched in the passenger's seat of the car. She was so tired. Tired of the colors and the smells and the noise. It was as though the place was never quiet.

She picked at the glitter on her pants, dropping pieces to the floor with the rest of the puddles shimmering there.

"I'd stay with you. I don't know Dad." Of course not. Serenity was too young when he left. "Why would he come back?"

"I don't know. Maybe he had problems to fix in himself. Maybe he wants to make amends."

"Amends?"

"Make up for doing something bad."

"Okay. So, he wants to show up and be part of our life. If he learns the rules, he could maybe stay with us for a little while? Until we figure out if we can handle being a family?"

"Ohana like in Lilo & Stitch?" Serenity asked.

"Yeah. We could work together. But if he just showed up one day and said that the courts said he could take you, but only if you agreed to go with him, what would you do?"

"Say 'no.'" There was no hesitation. "Miss Elsa is here. Bye, Mom. I love you."

"I love you too, Seri."

"Bee?"

"Hi, Mom."

"Are you coming home on time?"

"I am."

"How's the quest?"

"Punctuated boredom. These things always are. Mom, have I been sounding okay on the phone to you?"

"Yes, you sound like yourself. What's wrong? Are you drinking again?"

"No. Blue here drinks wine like it's water, but she's very good about not trying to press anything on me. I just, I'm not feeling like myself, so I figured I'd ask." She didn't feel like herself at all. She touched the knife on her hip. Oh, the jerky. Maybe she needed protein.

"It's the first time you've been away for a week. That's probably all it is."

"I guess. Mom. If this cure had some sort of cost, like, I'd never be able to touch Seri again, what would you say?"

"That it's Seri's decision, not ours. This is like when you asked me about the DNR I put on file. It's my decision. My life."

Tears caught in her throat. "I don't think I can talk about that right now, okay?"

"Oh, sweetheart. I love you very much. Never forget that." Blue waved from the doorway. She'd tied her end of the belt on. Time for walkies.

"I love you too. Okay, I've got to get going. I'll call tomorrow."

"Be careful out there and don't trust those doctors one bit."

"Oh, I don't."

Blue watched her put her phone away with a frown. "Is everything okay?" she asked as soon as she was in range.

"Just Mom stuff. I miss my daughter."

"I totally understand."

Bianka tied the belt around her own wrist. "Off to see the wizard then?"

"Dragon. Dragon. He probably is a wizard though. Most dragons of his age are. He's a brilliant mind."

"Do I sense a crush on your lawyer?"

"Don't even. He's much too old for me."

"Really? I wouldn't throw him out of the bed. That's for sure."

"Dragons don't date humans. That would be like you dating a cow or something equally edible."

Bianka shook her head. "You're insane. Off to see the old and not sexually active dragon because we don't want to think about his mating issues."

"Except I'll have to." Blue wrinkled her nose. "Thanks for the horrible reminder."

"I do my best." The Market had a surge of people at the front. It was like a Wal-Mart Black Friday crowd. They edged around against the arch and down the side that didn't have whatever deal that had attracted everyone's attention. "So, what sort of deal can cause that here? Specialized weapons?"

"New designer drugs." Blue's eyes traced over the crowd. "One tailored to dryads, I think. That's what most of those are. Oh, they must be selling fae opiates as well because the line of non-magical addicts is huge."

"If they're non-magical how did they end up here? People like me?"

"You can always find The Market if you really need it. A little LSD and the freedom to follow where it leads." Blue eyed the crowd. "Love to see what they're trying."

"Dragon. Lawyer."

"Right. Paperwork. Doesn't mean we can't have some fun along the way."

"It is when we need to get there on time."

Blue rolled her eyes. "I can control time, remember?"

"Yes, but if you do that, you can't actually go investigate what they're using, can you?"

The other woman looked at her. She blinked her ridiculously made up eyes. "How do you do that? Seriously, how do you manage to remember things like that? You've only seen me to it once."

"It was my first exposure to magic. It was memorable."

Blue shook her head. "Fine. Let's go." She led the way through the crowd. "Oooh, wait, there's a chocolate stand." She bought a large box of chocolates. She offered an actual Hershey's bar to Bianka. "Here. This is totally safe."

"Thank you." Bianka checked the security of the wrapper. It was still sealed. She savored the chocolate as they walked. Her eyes caught on two rather shifty eyed men who were watching Blue. The taller of the two was scarecrow thin with a straggly beard. The other was rib achingly thin. Their eyes were on the chocolate, she realized. She looked down with regret at the half a bar that was still intact. She wrapped it shut again and tossed it at them. The scarecrow caught it. He raised his brows in surprise. But he and his companion grinned at her. The smaller one tipped an imaginary hat. She nodded at him. "Time to go," she said through her teeth.

Blue closed the box. "Spoilsport." She shoved one of the truffles into her mouth. "You know what would go well with this? A nice red wine."

"Or, you could get some hot chocolate. Or coffee would work as well."

"There's the shortcut."

"Isn't there another way?"

"None that are this quick." The alley was as disturbing as the first time through. She felt Pink-moth-hamster trembling against her but didn't have a hand to comfort him while she was on guard for whatever was going to try to kill them there. She took deep, even breaths to keep her stomach intact as they exited. "I really don't know why you don't like it. It's just an alley."

"I can't believe you don't see any of the creepy crawlies that want to eat us when we go through there."

Blue just rolled her eyes.

"Don't look at me in that tone of voice." Bianka slapped a hand over her mouth. "I'm channeling my mother. That's horrible. When did I get old?"

The fairy laughed at her. "Motherhood does horrible things to your brain. I swear." The brownstone looked as simple as it had the day before, but Blue stood staring up at it. She was shivering and clutching at her box of chocolates. Bianka put her arm around her. "I'm getting everything I wanted. I'm terrified."

Bianka just held her more tightly. There was nothing to say to that.

Chapter 12

Linneas led them into the parlor. "I will bring tea," he said. There was a slight hesitation in his words. "Sweetened, Miss Blue?"

"Please."

"Some water would be lovely," Bianka said, pulling on the manners her mother had taught her.

"Of course." He gave them a shallow bow. He paused again. "I just wanted to say, thank you for helping with this reproduction business. It's very tricky. And Master cannot be out of circulation."

Blue's smile was bright. "You're very welcome, Linneas. I hope your master knows how good you are for him."

Linnaes' smile held a secret. "Thank you, ma'am."

Bianka gazed after him. "So Linneas and Draconis hmmm?"

"What are you? No, it's not like that." Blue bit at her lip. "Well maybe. You think?" Her eyes lit up with mischief. "That would be stellar. Do you think they've found another dragon to act as a surrogate and that's why they need my help?"

"I couldn't comment on the affairs of dragons. I am crunchy and taste okay with ketchup or barbecue sauce."

"A sound policy," Darconis said. "Though barbecue sauce is gauche. I'd use a salt and pepper mixture with a touch of cayenne."

"I'll keep that in mind." Bianka stood in greeting.

"Please, sit down. You'll want to be seated for this. Linnaes will have tea. And I've heard you enjoy sodas? I've a wonderfully dry one from Brazil. Guarana. It's rather like a Ginger Ale. Would you care to try it?"

"I hate to insist, but only if it's in its original packaging." Bianka sat next to Blue on the sofa. She tried not to think about already having a reputation in the market.

"Wise precaution." The walls of the room started to fade out. The glittering in the corners became more intense. Bianka gripped Blue's wrist. If they needed to bolt, she wouldn't have time to say anything. The walls faded out, leaving the furniture carefully situated amongst piles of gold, jewels, and object d' art. The painting that had been above the mantle sat on a pile of gold bars. Bianka stared around them.

"Wow," she managed.

"It is impressive isn't it?" Draconis beamed with understandable pride. "It's taken centuries. There's an entire library on the other side of the lair."

Then, Bianka looked up. The ceiling arched high above them. It looked like the inside of an amethyst geode that was almost twelve stories high. "Jessa Kest," she breathed. "I wish my daughter could see this. Just this morning she was giggling about my meeting a dragon instead of a doctor."

Draconis' smile was soft. "I fear that until you find her cure that is quite impossible. Though, if you figure a way to do it, I would welcome her in my home and at my table."

"Thank you." Bianka loosened her grip on Blue's wrist. Suddenly, she didn't feel nearly as nervous in front of the predator.

"I have the paperwork and the address for you, Periwinkle." He handed Blue a sheaf of actual parchment. The lettering was as beautiful as any calligraphy Bianka had ever seen. Blue studied the contract thoughtfully. She read through all of the papers while Linneas returned and poured the tea for her. He offered her an unopened can of soda to look over It felt real, looked real, and read real, so she opened it and poured it into the offered glass.

"Thank you. Oh, this is wonderful," she said to Draconis. "I need to see if I can find this somewhere. Maybe the bar supplier could get it. It would be good to discretely cut people off with."

"You tend bar, then?"

"Yes."

"Yet you don't partake. How incredible. Rumor has it you managed to indebt two Hellhounds today. You are a remarkable woman."

"Hellhounds? No, I tossed some chocolate to a couple of homeless guys who were scoping Blue out as a target for mugging."

The dragon chuckled. "As I said, a remarkable woman."

"Everything seems to be in order." Blue tucked them away into the spangled messenger bag she wore instead of a purse.

"Good, then you understand that payment must be made."

"Yes." Blue grimaced. "I don't know how long this reproduction takes though."

"Five months at the outside. Your bubble will need to be able to include Linneas and myself. Of course, Bee will be able to remain at your side."

"Wait, you're going to do this now? I can't be away from Serenity for five months."

Blue rolled her eyes. "Remember what we were talking about? My magic means that it won't be five months. It won't even be five minutes more. And then, you'll be able to drag me back to the hotel and tomorrow we'll find the cure for your daughter."

"And while you're holding the bubble, I'll be doing what? Reading through the library?"

"That would be a good idea. You do have some talent in bending the world to your way of thinking." Draconis nodded slowly. "In fact, you've created magic so powerful that Periwinkle's name is not currently Periwinkle. In fact, it's more than Blue Jones. I would wager that no one using her real name can currently track her."

Bianka was never, never going to tell them that it was still 'Blue-glitter-red-wine.' She blushed at the thought. "No, it's not Blue Jones."

Blue giggled. "I want to know what it is, but later. Much later. Okay, so I take these papers to my daughter and she gets the option of signing them. They'll file themselves?"

"Yes."

"And the reproduction will happen in the lair?"

"Yes."

"I can do that. Do you have enough food for all of us though? And is it all safe for Bee?"

Linneas cleared his throat. "I assume that your magic does not interfere with magic lockers?"

"I don't know. It'll be frozen in the second with us and magic isn't instant, so it will keep things cold, but it won't be able to draw anything from someplace else." Blue tapped at her teeth.

"Then, I cannot confirm that we are completely prepared. However, Miss Bee and myself will be able to leave the confines of the lair. I will provide Miss Bee with credit slips to leave with whichever merchants she chooses to custom with." Linnaes stood steadily next to Draconis. Yes, they were partners. There was no question.

"And how do I find these merchants?" Bianka was not going to just go along with this.

"You must keep your mind focused on what you wish to find. Then, your attention will guide you." The dragon cocked his head to the side. "Did no one explain the nature of The Market?"

"I was told that whatever I needed I could find it at The Market."

"Very true. And you will be alerted to what you need."

Bianka considered for a moment. "What I need." She stressed the last word. "Which may not be the same as what I want." She nodded slowly. She resisted the urge to touch the knife on her hip. Protection, a way to hold on to Blue and keep her hands free, a pet to guide her home that looked like an anime creature, a ribbon to do what she needed with, ginger ale that was safe to drink, and chocolate that was from home. "Five months is a long time to go without talking to my daughter."

"You wouldn't leave me all alone, would you?" Blue turned large, wet eyes on her.

"No, I promised you a week." She grimaced. "But I could step out of the bubble and be put to sleep with the rest."

"No, I don't want to take off the belt until we're safely in the bubble. If the Court really can't track me, then it means my husband can't either and no one will know that I was meeting with Draconis."

Shit. When it was put that way, she couldn't in good conscience refuse. She'd promised to protect Blue and she was being protected from her husband by Bianka just being there? "Okay. Fine. How do we do this?"

Blue grinned. "Everyone ready?"

"Are you comfortable? Five months is a long time and if I remember the coffee shop properly, you won't be able to move."

The fairy grimaced. "I've never held it for that long. I don't know." She bit at her lip. "I think the armchair is better. And we can turn it so I'm not staring at Mr. Draconis the entire time."

"I'm much more vain that you think," Draconis stated. "I'll transform once you've started the bubble."

Blue settled in the armchair with an exaggerated wiggle. Her skirt puffed up over the arms and spilled blue glitter down the sides of it. What a horrible thing to do to such a pretty chair. Bianka stood next to her, one hand on her shoulder. "You're sure about this?"

"Positive. Payment for services rendered." She waved a hand and a flash of glitter covered the floor in front of her. "There we go. All stopped."

Draconis nodded. He stepped back and started to change form. There was no glitter or gold. Instead, his face lengthened and grew until he had a dragon's head on a human body, small horns peering out from behind his ears and ridges of bone over his dark eyes. Then, his body shifted slowly, until he was a staggering three stories tall with wings large enough and powerful enough to lift his body. A curl of smoke drifted from his nostrils. His purple scales shimmered like faceted jewels. A gold medallion hung the size of a platter around his neck.

Linnaes looked up with a brilliant smile that showed off his sharp white teeth. Two dragons. Of course, they were both dragons. His face lengthened, though his snout was smaller. He was about half Draconis' size, with ebony scales and a matching necklace. "My wife is very beautiful isn't she, Miss Bee?"

"Wife?" Oh, how embarrassing. Assumptions. And Draconis had done nothing to contradict their assumptions. That was just cruel. "She is," Bianka confirmed. "Though very attractive in human form as well."

"I've always thought so," Linnaes said. "Miss Periwinkle, thank you for giving us this opportunity. We've wanted a child for years."

"You're very welcome." Blue's voice was faint. "Bee, can you find a mirror? I think I might actually want to see them as themselves."

"Sure." Linnaes pointed out a mirror that was large enough to see them in, but small enough for her to move on her own. "Here, Lady of Shallot, see what's going on behind you." She set the mirror against the "mantle" wall.

"Oh, you're both beautiful," Blue said. She was blushing. "I'm so sorry, I assumed."

"You were meant to. I've been Andre Draconis for centuries. A human and a young fairy would never see through that illusion." Androgynous dragons. What a concept.

Bianka considered the untied belt. "You'll be okay if I go exploring? I really think these two need me to not be staring at them," she murmured. "I'll go hunt down some food."

"Bring me wine. Lots and lots of wine."

Linnaes chuckled. "There's a stack of credit slips on the table near the door. Please, use them for whatever you need. Just give me an accounting when you come back."

"Of course." Bianka smiled at them all before escaping with a stack of parchment and nightmare visions of watching dragon sex. There were things in this world that should remain mysteries.

Chapter 13

The Market didn't have the strange blue cast that the coffee shop had. In fact, there was still movement. The people weren't moving at all. They were all frozen in place. It was eerily quiet. The thrum of noise that seemed to constantly run through the streets was gone, but they still pulsed with the beat. She could feel it traveling through her chest, like a sub-woofer gone mad. She set off to find food and drinks. She grimaced, considering the problem of supplying Blue with wine. She drank gallons of the stuff. It couldn't be healthy no matter what sort of sugar it contained.

So, sodas and maybe seltzer water to mix with white wines and fruit to put into it. She really wanted access to something like Harris Teeter, not little shops that she didn't recognize. Maybe she should go back to the hotel and stock up on what was in those cabinets. She looked at the alley. No way. Not when she didn't have to. The pink-moth-hamster shifted under her shirt and she looked down at it. "Hey, kiddo, do you need something special? Or should I just keep feeding you sugar water?" He moved up to rest against her neck. She stroked his warm fur. "You're just the cutest thing. I swear. If Serenity catches a glimpse of you, you'll never have any rest. If you see something you need, you just go fly to it, okay."

She felt something like child's laughter against her chin and assumed that was an agreement. "So, you can communicate. I guess it just hasn't been quiet enough, huh?" She rubbed a finger along her head. "Food and drinks first. Then, I can find something to keep me from going crazy. It's too late for Blue."

She picked her way past the people in the street. The walls of the buildings pulsed with color and patterns. Pictures scattered across the ground and on people's skin. There were people of all shades in the streets. More colors than she'd noticed before. A rainbow of glitter hung in the air like fireworks trapped in glass.

Stalls flickered in and out of being. The ones she saw were food booths with skewers of meat and beer flowing freely. She tapped her foot, thinking. She focused on wanting prepackaged food that didn't need cooking. A stall of camping equipment flickered into being.

She selected a bulk box of meals that came with their own heaters, then added a camp-stove and fuel to the pile. She wrote out a careful credit slip and made a note for Linnaes. This might be easier than she'd thought. She turned to return to the house, then stopped as a horrified thought popping up. What if they were still... negotiating the reproduction? No, she was not stepping foot inside the house until she could be sure they'd finished. Wine and soda next. And maybe some candy. Or hot chocolate mix.

When she turned, she saw the two men she'd fed earlier. They still looked chronically underfed. Surrounded by anything they could want, and still starving. It was like those two years she'd spent on the street looking for her next fix. She took two of the meals out of the box and tucked one into each man's pants. At least they could get one meal before they needed their next fix. Though it was odd that they were nearby. Had she and Blue actually been followed? The alley was too distracting to notice if someone else were in it and not an immediate threat.

"We need to find a wine shop. And maybe a pub or something," she said to Pink-moth-hamster. "And you really need a name, so I don't feel like I'm talking to myself."

The hair on the back of her neck stood up. She looked around. Sound was starting to creep in all around her. It wasn't the overwhelming sound of walking into The Market. It was voices just out of the room and a dance-track muffled by a sweater. She could almost taste the purple that was running along the street in waves. It was bitter and sharp like bile after your hangover had emptied everything out of your stomach and you were stuck heaving out whatever acids your body could create.

She let it sweep over her feet. "This is the longest flashback I have ever had, pink-moth-hamster dear." He rubbed his ears against her chin.

//love//

She froze. "That was definitely communication if not actual words. Try again."

//hunger//

"Okay, let's find something for you to eat then. Soda?"

//assent//

She focused on a nice cold ginger ale. The wine shop popped into her head and she started walking. It was a long way to the actual cross-street rather than the alley in order to get back to the entrance she knew. She was not taking the alley. Not unless Blue was pulling on her wrist and quivering with over-sugared enthusiasm at her. A vending machine was propped casually against the wall. She stared at it. Then, she stepped forward and pressed the button to see how much it was charging for its old-school cans. "Okay, I'm not going to argue with good luck." She dug out the beaded cat-head coin purse that her daughter had given her for her birthday.

She had three cans in her box and one open. She took a long gulp, then poured some into the palm of her hand and let her pet drink it. "More?"

//assent//

She fed it almost half a can before he sent //sated// at her. "You have no idea how long it's been since I actually felt that way," she informed him. "I mean, I haven't had a hook-up since Serenity's father left."

//ew//

"So, you don't want to hear about my lack of sex life. Fair enough." She finished off the can and tossed it onto a scrap metal pile that was next to the machine. "Still have to find some wine for the glittery one."

She shouldered her way into the brownstone with a full box of meals and wine. "Everyone decent in here?" she called before turning her head.

Linneas and Draconis laughed at her. "It is not nearly as messy for us as it is for a human."

"Mercifully short. Where's my wine?" Blue glared at her.

"Maybe I couldn't find any."

"Don't make me sick Linneas on you. He doesn't have any tolerance for the way I whine."

"Thankfully, I do. In fact, I don't like your attitude, young lady."

Blue's mouth snapped shut and she sat up as much as possible. "I'm sorry. May I please have some wine, Bee?"

"Better." Bianka handed her a bottle. "I'm sure there's a glass around here."

Blue laughed at her, opened the bottle by waving a finger over it. "And there you have one of the few tricks I have." She tipped the bottle into her mouth. "Oh, this is good. Fruity and sweet."

"Strawberry wine. I recognized the vintner." Bianka set down the box. "I've got that accounting here for you, Linneas. Where should I put it?"

"Just hand it here." The dark dragon put out his paw. She settled the parchment in his hand. He lifted it up to peer at it, adjusting a pair of reading glasses. It was the glasses that made her have to turn around and take deep breaths. Her mother would kill her if she were rude to someone in their own home. And her mother would know somehow. It was like a sixth sense or something.

"Pink-moth-hamster, started communicating with me," she told Blue. "Basically, just when he's hungry, but it's working."

Blue smiled. She reached out a hand and Bianka came close enough for her to pet the little creature who was not letting go of her. "He's adorable. Has he told you his name yet?"

"Not unless his name is 'hungry.'"

Blue laughed. "Sit, tell me what it's like out there."

Linneas poked his large head into the human scaled area. "You will need more than this, I'm sure. When I said anything you need, I meant it."

"I don't need much. We'll renew the food stores when we need to. It should hold Blue and me for a while. I don't know what you two need though."

"I will come shopping with you to supply us with fresh meat. Andre will need more than usual because she's conceived."

"Just once and bam baby? I don't know whether to be pleased for you or horrified." Blue looked at him with a confused face. "It took a lot more time with my kids. Bee?"

"I forgot protection once and bam, baby," she deadpanned. "Condoms are your friend."

Linneas just looked between them. He cocked his head to the side. "It takes multiple matings for you to conceive. Can't you control your eggs?"

"Doesn't work that way for humans. Once a month we produce an egg."

"Fairies constantly have eggs, but the boys aren't always fertile," Blue explained. She glanced at Bianka. "You really won the lottery with your boy."

Bianka snorted out a laugh. "If he'd only stuck around, I'd agree with you." Nate had done her some good. He'd helped her get into rehab and back into school. Maybe, maybe if they hadn't made Serenity he'd still be at her side and explaining all the politics of Fairyland. She let the thought go. She wouldn't give up Serenity for anyone.

Chapter 14

"Come on, Chappy, let's go make Blue's spritzer." The pink-moth-hamster - now named Schiaparelli in honor of the designer - flew to her side and perched on her shoulder. He rubbed his furry head against her cheek.

"You're watering down the wine," Blue complained. That was completely true. Bianka had started watering down the wine as soon as she could. Two months had made a difference. Blue was down from ten bottles a day to five bottles a day. Not that she really noticed. The amount of sweets and colas she drank had increased to balance out the loss of calories.

//you mean?// Chappy asked.

"It's for her own good," she murmured. "I want her to remember she has a daughter."

//Blue silly.//

"Yes, she is."

"Is that moth bad-mouthing me again?" Blue demanded.

"I have no idea what you're talking about. You're getting paranoid."

"It's not paranoia if they're out to get me." Draconis flicked a coin at the back of her head. "Damn it, Dragon!" She shook the gold coin out of her hair. "When I get out of this chair, I'll..."

"You'll what?"

"I'll tell everyone that you actually prefer schnapps to scale rub!"

"Oh, that's a good one," Linnaes said. He was snuggled against his wife's side, listening to the baby. Bianka had been expecting an egg and a nest, but dragons were one of the few species that had live births. The biology major that her head wanted to be was twitching about all the fascinating possibilities there were in cryptozoology.

Bianka handed Blue the white wine spritzer. "Lin, did you want to come out with me today?"

"You're abandoning me with them? After the appalling tiddly-winks situation?"

"You started that one. And I found a top hat for you to throw cards into. Or did you want a book before I go out?"

"I'll take a book in case I get tired of learning to throw cards. I'm not a stage magician you know. I don't need those tricks."

"But it's fun and you're getting better and better."

"True." Blue sipped the spritzer. "You're trying to make me get sober, aren't you?"

"What part of my transparent ploy have you noticed?"

"The fact that you won't get me any pills."

Bianka sniffed. "I'm not company enough?"

"Shove it in a sock. I'm so bored."

"Wow. I've just had a flash of what the teenage years are going to be like. Book?"

"Please. Something on business law maybe."

"I'll fetch one for you," Linnaes said. "I know where everything in the library is. Have a good walk, Bee."

Bianka stretched. "I need a workout. And then, I have to do something about my hair, Chappy. It's getting a little too long." Her hair had grown out and her daughter would notice. She could see the brown roots. "It'd be nice to not have to worry about it. Blue's highlights are her real color, lucky thing."

The throbbing street welcomed her. The shifting colors were yellow today and tasted like Starburst candy. The first flicker in the corner of her eye made her think there was just was something wrong with her eyes. She'd gotten used to the constantly shifting pictures and the throbbing waves of colors. This was black. As black as her outfit and stood out just as badly.

"Chappy?" The pink-moth-hamster had curled up in her cleavage the way he hadn't since the beginning of the bubble.

He chirped at her. That was not comforting at all.

The flicker of black slid along the nearest wall like a solid shadow. Nothing was supposed to be moving. Had Blue missed something? She let her hands fall into loose fists and she started scanning the street, her shoulders bunched up. The black thing extended a quick arm toward her. She dodged it and it bounced off of one of the frozen walkers.

Okay, so it couldn't hurt them. Did that mean it couldn't hurt her? Another tendril extended and she used a man the size of an elephant as a shield. She glanced toward the brownstone. No, she couldn't bring whatever this was back. Draconis was pregnant and Blue was stuck in place. She bolted down the road. "Why the fuck did I stop jogging?" she asked.

//silly//

"That was rhetorical."

//human prey//

"Caught that."

She bolted into the bright red doors of the closest pub. The entire place inside was lit up flame red. All six surfaces of the room. She took a deep breath. She looked around the room. Half the people were sprawled out on the floor in the midst of an orgy. Okay, she obviously had this door confused with some other red room she'd been in. She didn't want to stay. Not when there was something hunting that was supposed to be asleep. She went out the back door and stopped on the threshold to get her bearings. She'd never seen this part of The Market before.

The buildings were more ornate and less human. There was a towering spiral of glass in the center of the street instead of a fountain and gouts of gold flooded from it. She looked closer to realize that the gold was actually scotch. She had somehow stumbled into the drug part of the market. She huffed out a laugh. "I guess I needed a drink." She shook her head. She was not going to be that weak, although right now a glass of scotch sounded nice. Familiar. Safe.

She had to run. There were two black things sliding over the crystal surfaces of the buildings. The buildings glistened like ice. One of the creatures sent out a tendril in her direction. She darted across the street and into the shadow of the fountain. Such a waste of good alcohol.

//sober//

"Shut up you little rat."

//amusement//

"I wish I could curl up in someone's bra right now." She ran for the far end of the street in the opposite direction of the shadows. What were they? why had she never seen them before?

Oh shit, there was one right in front of her. She didn't have time to think. She grabbed her knife and threw at its mass. There was a high-pitched keening before the tendrils pulled back. It writhed, pinned against the building. Other shadows slipped toward it.

Should she stay or run? She stilled, pretending to be frozen, just watching. They rippled around the shadow but didn't seem to be doing anything. The keening echoed and built and then faded into the thumping she was used to feeling beneath her feet. The shadows slipped away, leaving a grey trail on the wall. She edged toward it. She pulled her knife free of the wall. It was coated in ichor. She wiped it off on one of the sleeping drunks at the mouth of the closest alley, then sheathed her knife.

"Well, that was exciting."

She looked mournfully at a patch of spilled, blue and white pills. She didn't know what they were, but they called to her. Her fingers shook.

//SOBER//

"I know. I know." She lifted her chin and strode by the pills as though she'd never considered picking one up. "Who appointed you my conscience anyway?"

//torture blue//

She snorted. "You are a twisted, little freak and I love you."

//love// The pink-moth-hamster assured her. He didn't leave her shirt though. Her nerves jangled and pills and drinks called to her as she passed. She needed to find a way out of this part of town fast. Someplace quiet and safe. A shimmering orange door appeared in front of her. She yanked it open and stepped into the library. She curled up in the corner by the door as tears started to stream down her face.

Her pet crawled up to sit on her shoulder. He crooned at her while she sobbed.

Chapter 15

Bianka finished the little nest of coins off with a nice hand-knotted Oriental rug. She nodded once, then curled up in it and flipped an antique quilt over herself from her head to her feet. She peered out from the little slit she left to survey the room. The rug was soft, but the coins were not. She shifted until she was comfortable, then closed her eyes. The pink-moth-hamster curled up at the mouth of her little burrito cave and watched the room, while he occasionally rubbed against her forehead. She fell asleep.

It was nearly a day later when Linneas' large eye peered into her nest. "Are you coming out of there today? I'm not sure how much water to put into the wine today."

"Half a glass of ginger ale in white wine," she told him.

"But are you coming out?"

"Nope. I'm a dragon now. I'm hibernating and you don't want to disturb me."

Draconis snorted at that somewhere above her head. Linneas changed into his human form. He lay down so that he could look into her eyes. Something in her heart clenched a little and there were tears in her throat. "Is this about the Time-Meister blood I smelled?"

"Time-Meister? What Time-Meister?" Blue demanded from her chair. It wasn't that far away from the nest. Bianka couldn't not watch over her.

"Is that what that thing was?"

Draconis rested her head on Bianka's back with delicacy that her size decried. "Oh, poor Bee. Did one of them touch you?"

"Those black octopus type things that wanted to eat me? No. I ducked."

Linneas slowly reached forward until he was touching her hand. "And the blood?"

"I pinned one to the wall." Her breathing sped up. She started to shake. Chappy snuggled against her throat. Linneas tightened his grip around her hand. "The others took it away. What are they? Why didn't you warn me about them?"

"They don't go after human prey. At least I didn't think so." Linneas grimaced. "They live outside time, through time, in all times and in none. They eat memories and broken timelines. They also feast on the weaker of their own kind."

"So why come after me? Do they think I'm something that got lost? Do I look like their prey?"

"I don't really know that much about them. I've never seen one myself, just smelled them," Draconis answered her. "Periwinkle, perhaps you know?"

"I've never heard of one trying for a human. I'm sure there's at least one person who's gotten trapped out of time."

"I might have a book on the creatures. Allow me to look." Bianka turned her hand around to grab his wrist. He bit his lip the relaxed against the gold, though it had to be uncomfortable for him. "Later. After you've had something to eat. You used your dagger to pierce one? May I see your weapon?"

She presented the knife but didn't let go of his hand or the knife. "Blue got it for me the first day we were here."

Linneas' tongue flicked out. It was quick and forked like a snake, even in human form. It touched the metal briefly. "Meteorite with silver ore. An excellent weapon. And one that many fae could not touch." He nodded. "There is a theory that Time-Meisters are fae related."

"Because they manipulate time?"

"They don't manipulate anything. They are simple creatures. They have no agendas, simply hunger. And they will eat those things that time disposes of. Ghosts, remnants of timelines thrown aside by choices. Ones made redundant and collapsed. Memories forgotten or thrown aside. The detritus of life. Scavengers."

"So, I was nearly eaten by a time starfish. Wonderful. I'm staying in here for the day. Deal with it."

"Very well." She let Linnaes pull back. "I'll bring you something to eat."

"I am not too heavy?" Draconis asked.

"Not at all." It was nice. Like having her mother tuck her in or sit with her when she was ill. The shakes receded. She lay her head down after sheathing her knife. Her eyes closed against images of the black tendrils finding their way into the lair. This was the bubble though. She had no idea what they'd make of it.

Linnaes brought her a cup of tea, a bottle of soda, beef jerky, and something that was heated up from the box of camp supplies. It smelled Italian. She ate everything he brought her while tasting none of it. The world had greyed out. Nothing existed beyond her little cave. At least, not until the books arrived.

They were large tomes, as thick as the phone book and as large as an atlas. They were bound in animal hide with large brass clasps on them to keep them shut. She could smell the glue and the dust. These were old-school books. She reached out a hand and traced over the embossed lettering. "A Guide to Fae Creatures," the first one read. "The Focus of Will," was the next. "Who's Who in the Fairy Court," in contrast was a modern style trade paperback.

"You're killing me here," she said.

Linneas grinned at her. "You'll have to sit up to read them."

"I'm really hating you now."

Draconis laughed. It rolled along her back. "Come on, Busy Bee." The large dragon's head lifted.

Bianka could hear her mother in those words. It took her back to a time before she had a child. Before the drugs and the alcohol and the yearning to just be normal damn it. She was too smart and too brown for that to ever happen. The alcohol was just at parties first, and then it just started to spiral out of control until she was an addict on the streets. She'd met Serenity's father and got clean. He'd pursued her for more than a year. She tried to reach for the innocent feeling of childhood, but it slipped away like a Jell-O-shot.

She pushed herself up, letting the blanket linger around her shoulders like a cape. She popped the top of the Coke and dragged the largest book toward her. "Should I be wearing gloves or something?"

"No, no, I've put archivists' spells on all of it. You could spill wine on it, and it wouldn't be damaged."

"I know a librarian or two who'd kill for that ability." She opened the clasp, then carefully lifted the cover. It was fully illustrated in hand-drawn pictures. Her breath caught. "This is beautiful."

"The fae are beautiful, but dangerous. The older they are, the more powerful they become," Blue warned. "You know, like me, if someone doesn't get me some more damned wine!"

"I've got it here."

"Watch your tone of voice, Missy," Bianka said absently.

"You're not my real Mom," Blue sassed back.

Bianka looked up and narrowed her eyes at the fairy. Blue stuck her tongue out but gave Linnaes a genuine smile and thank-you for his trouble. "Good girl," she praised.

Blue presented her middle finger.

"Children these days," Draconis sniffed. "I really don't know what I was thinking."

Blue snorted at that. "I'm sure you'll have a sweetheart of a child with a lawyer's mind and the theatricality of a stage magician." Her voice echoed around the room and into the soaring rafters overhead. She swallowed, eyes getting wide. "Um, and I might have just inadvertently made myself it's fairy godmother."

"That is very sweet of you. Thank you," Draconis said.

"So, this force of will book. Is this supposed to be some form of English or is it Arabic?" Bianka's brows knitted together. "I can read about three words in Arabic."

"It's English. Mixed with runes and a few other letters." Linnaes looked at the book. "Oh, it's in mirror-script. There's a hand-mirror around here somewhere." He dove into a pile of treasures that clinked as he moved them.

"Or she could just come over here and look in the big mirror she set up for me."

Bianka considered for a moment. "That might be better. And I really should get up. I guess." Chappy chirped at her and snuggled into her cleavage. "I'm not sure if you're sweet or lecherous at this point."

//Love.//

"Oh, don't try that old line on me."

//Pleasure. Amusement.//

Bianka groaned as she stood up. "That may have been a mistake."

"Standing up? Or cocooning yourself in the middle of a gold pile as opposed to over here on the couch?"

"I can't make a good burrito over on the couch. I used to watch cartoons where you could swim in gold coins. I'm terribly disappointed at the reality."

"That sounds like something that would take a good magician to do." The fairy sipped her wine. "I am holding the fact that you're weaning me onto sodas against you. Alcohol has a very high sugar content."

"Be nice and I'll find the ice cream again."

"Phish food this time? Please? I will be the sweetest little fae you ever did meet."

"Two days. No whining and I'll get the ice cream."

"Deal."

Bianka dove into the book, sipping absently at the ginger ale that Linnaes set near her hand. She caught the edge of a shared smile between him and Blue but didn't look away from the reflected page. The force of will is what separates the human sorcerer from the fae. The fae need only think and their magic will supply their needs, so long as they are sufficiently powerful. The human sorcerer will need to concentrate and shape the magic to his will. She frowned at the book and the complex diagrams for ritual spells.

"This seems wrong to me," she said. "If I could rename Blue without concentrating on the idea, why would I need to do anything this complex?"

"You are not a man," Draconis stated. "You'll need one of the grimoires."

Linnaes frowned. "What grimoires? You traded the last one back to the Rosanna Petrova for the protection potion for the windows."

"That was the last Romany one. There's an American herbal around here. It's not a grimoire proper. But I think it'll suit better." Draconis shifted and there was a tumble of gold coins and jewels. A crown settled near her front foot. She poked at it with a talon. "Come here, Busy Bee."

Bianka picked up the crown. It was a child's tiara of plastic and rhinestones. She bit her lip. It was something that Serenity could never have. The rhinestones were backed in metal and the combs to hold it on were aluminum. Draconis tapped Bianka on the head.

"Put it on."

Bianka quirked a semi-sweet smile at her. She placed it on her head.

"I dub thee queen of the bubble with power over all you survey outside of these walls."

Something strange tingled through her fingers. She straightened up quickly. "I thank thee, milady." A rush of memories from the fantasy novels that had gotten her through high school bubbled up. Magic worked differently in every one of them. Maybe even inside the bubble worked differently than in the Market. "Where would I find the American books?"

"Just here," Linnaes pointed at the shelf he was next to. "You'll want to look through them yourself." She moved to the shelf. "Just remember that not every book is the right fit for the reader."

"Right."

Chapter 16

Bianka stood at the door of the row-house. She'd avoided going out for a full week. She couldn't do it any longer. They needed food. They needed wine. Blue was still going through an alarming amount, though it was less every week. Soon, she'd be feeding her just plain sodas in between glasses of wine. "It's not going to open for you," Blue said. Bianka flipped her off. The fairy giggled. "So not my type. Sorry, sweetie."

Bianka pulled open the door like yanking off a bandage. She took a deep breath, then stepped out into the street. She shut the door behind herself before she could chicken out. Chappy rubbed against her chin, then settled into his favorite place in her shirt. "I swear, you are a letch."

//Agreement.//

She snorted. She gripped her knife and forced her foot to move. Soon, they were out in the street. She could see the Time-Meisters more clearly. They were questing through the bubble poking at everything in the street. She closed her eyes and took one breath, then another. She pulled out Serenity's picture and stared at it. She wanted nothing more than to wrap her arms around her daughter and hold her.

//Questioning.// Chappy interrupted. He nosed against the picture.

"This is my daughter," she told him. "Serenity. I'm here to cure her." It was as much for her benefit as his. She could put up with anything to save her daughter, but sometimes she just needed to be reminded of it. "Okay, let's do this."

Chappy rubbed her chin. She stroked his head with a finger. The first step onto the street seemed to echo through the street. The Time-Meisters froze. She stepped toward one of them. It retreated. Her laughter rang off of the walls from sheer joy. "So, what sort of food do you want, sweetie?"

//Sweet.// She nodded decisively.

She ended up dragging home cases of red wine and leaving them on the front porch after tucking one bottle into the bag of her hobo friends. She followed that up with stacks of beef jerky and soda. She finally dropped the last boxes of food on the steps before she flopped down next to them. She poured a capful of soda for Chappy to drink. She drank deeply. "I need to get my hair done," she informed her pet. He ignored her. "To make sure it matches you." That made him perk up. "Thought you'd like that, you vain little critter."

//Agreement.//

She stroked his head and he settle back between her breasts. "A little human contact wouldn't be a bad thing either." She pushed herself up to her feet and ventured back into the market. "Now where do you think I'll find a hairstylist, hmm?" She wandered through quiet streets – disco strobe lights followed her for a block, then dissipated. She eyed the walls for a moment, but there seemed to be nothing there. A black tendril from a Time-Meister curled away from her feet. It was great, but also disconcerting to have the time-starfish so frightened of her. It indicated a greater amount of sapience than she'd assumed from the description.

The sound of distant conversation caught her attention and she moved toward it. Then, she smelled hair relaxer and dye. She hurried toward the hair shop. "Don't you dare disappear on me."

The hair shop was filled with sound and smell and light, but no movement. It was as frozen as everything else. Then, everything seemed to snap back in to focus. Did that mean the time bubble was finished? But Blue wouldn't release it without her. "Oh, sweetie, you look like a woman in need of a little talkin'." The large woman behind the counter had the dark skin that Bianka's grandmother had and the same deep brown eyes. Her wrist was covered with a clash of metal bangles that shimmered and clattered as she moved. "What else can I get for you while we're talkin'?" She moved from behind the counter and offered her hand. "I'm Dee."

Bianka smiled automatically. "Hi, I'm Bee."

Dee laughed. "And what do you need today, Bee?"

"I need to cut this mess and refresh my pink."

"Then sit down and tell me your troubles."

Bianka settled in the chair and let the familiarity wash over her. She chatted cheerfully about her daughter complaining about bedtimes and her mother wanting her to get married. She even talked about the louts at work and not having enough tips coming in. About a boyfriend who abandoned her in the middle of the night when she was at the hospital with her baby. She didn't talk about dragons, or fairies, or time-starfish.

Dee cooed over Chappy and set out a dish of soda for him to lap at while the dye was setting. "He is adorable."

//Assent.//

"He agrees." Bianka couldn't help herself. She stroked down his back and he fluffed up happily at the contact.

"You're very lucky. They usually only stay with people for about a week. Now, this ex-boyfriend of yours. What was his name again?"

"Nate. Nate Palmer." She snorted. "At least that's the name I knew him by. At this point, I'm not sure he wasn't just trying to use me as cover." She was bitter. She knew she was bitter, but that wasn't something she could make herself forget. "I loved the bastard." She paused. "Love," she corrected herself. "Emotions don't just stop. I wouldn't be this mad at him if I didn't still love him."

Dee nodded. "Very true." The shop around them seemed to have movement and sound, but Bianka noticed that only she and Dee were in the same moment together. Everything else was just off in the distance. "Now, Queen Bee, I think I have something you just need to see." Bianka raised her brows as the other woman went to the front desk and returned with a magazine. "Now, I'm not one to gossip," Dee lied with a grin, "but check out the second page." She held out what seemed to be Fairyland's answer to People or maybe it was The Globe. It was flimsy in her hands, but the second page riveted her attention.

"Knight Pomegranate found guilty of breaking his vow to the Queen and starting a family. This is the second time Knight Pomegranate has been found in contempt of his vows. Will he survive a third strike?" The picture was Nate. Her Nate was a knight. And he had another child somewhere. And probably another ex-girlfriend, given that he apparently was supposed to be some sort of monk.

Dee sighed. "That's your Nate then?"

"Oh yes. I'd recognize that crooked little scar on his neck anywhere."

"Oh honey," Dee offered her arms. Bianka touched her cheek in surprise. It was wet. She let herself be hugged close. Dee offered no lies to try to comfort her, just a firm hug. "Now, let's get that foil out of your hair so you can get back out there and rule your realm. You'll match your little furry friend here."

Chappy wriggled happily at that. //Pleasure.// Bee had to laugh.

Chapter 17

It turned out that baby dragons were just as cute as baby anything else. After about a day, when Andrea and Linnaeus were sure the baby was properly imprinted, they were more than happy to let Blue hold and pet her godchild. The baby was a pastel purple blue with shimmering pink eyes and wings that weren't yet ready to hold its weight. It chirped for food like a baby bird and curled up like a kitten at random moments when it was tired. Though tired, Blue refused to let the bubble go until three days after the birth.

"I remember what it was like when I had my kids," she said. "I was exhausted for at least a week, but at least I had help. You get a day or two while Bee and I coo over our new little darling here. Who's a cutie?" she asked rubbing under the baby's chin with the back of her finger.

Bianka on the other hand was helping Linnaeus cut up meat for the baby. "Normally," he told her, "in the old days, a father would just drop a carcass into the lair and let the baby just gnaw on it. If this were fresh meat, I'd do just that, but it's already been processed, and I'd prefer it smell of me or you than some random stranger out there."

"Babies have a strong sense of smell?"

"Oh yes. And they'll associate the smell of the person who gave them food with safety. That's why there was such a dragon-napping craze a few centuries ago. The fairy knights figured out that the babies were impressionable. They soon came to regret it when they found out that dragons are strong-willed and dislike being put under reins, but that was their own fault now wasn't it?"

"So, I should really be wearing gloves when I handle the meat, so that it has your scent on it?"

Linnaeus smiled, teeth shining in the light. "Bianka, you are always welcome in our home and at our table. Without even thinking about it, you brought home meat for us as well as food for yourself and Blue. You've allowed me more time with my mate than most males ever get. I would have been hunting constantly for months to feed Andre and myself. You have provided companionship and were completely unafraid of my wife's crankiness. If at any time you need a place to stay, please consider this your home." He leaned against her shoulder with his own. "We'll even build you your own mini-lair of blankets and gold so that you can be a hibernating dragon."

Bianka blushed at the gentle teasing. "Thank you." She handed the plate of meat she was working on to him. "Do you know anything about Knight Pomegranate?"

The dragon blinked slowly. "He's in all the scandal papers right now. There are rumors that he's had an affair with a court lady. I'm afraid I couldn't confirm if that is true or not. He is handsome and treats most fairly. But he is his queen's vassal and hands, so he's also not available."

"He's a slut!" Blue called over her shoulder.

Linnaeus shook his head. "As are all fairies," he murmured for Bianka's ears only. "Pollinating everywhere. Will you be able to stay for the naming ceremony? Or perhaps come back for it, if you must go?"

"I don't know. That will depend on Blue and how long it takes to finish her business. And of course, on when it is."

"It will be in two months. We need to give the family time to gather." He frowned. "I know, I'll make up something for you to take as a reminder. It will tell you when the ceremony is and give you a path to get here. I would say to bring your daughter, but there will be a lot of metal around at the ceremony and I don't know how she'll react to gold."

"Badly. Steel and iron are the worst. Even surgical steel. Maybe especially surgical steel. We think platinum is maybe safe, but only in an emergency." Bianka frowned. "We've never tested gold or silver. We've just been busy avoiding it."

The dragon mulled that over while he went to set up the baby's feeding corner. He changed into his dragon form and coaxed his daughter to the food. Bianka settled on the arm of Blue's chair. The fairy leaned against her. They both needed the physical contact. Blue had been stuck in her chair for months.

"Will you need time to heal?" Bianka asked her bluntly. "Should I go find a wheelchair?"

Blue blinked. "I've never held a bubble for this long. I honestly don't know. My legs seem to work." She kicked out her skirt a bit. "They don't feel strange, but I don't know. Maybe a cane? Just in case?"

"Right. I'll just go shopping then." She kissed Blue's hair. "Be good. And don't spoil the baby too badly."

"But she's going to be intelligent and overly dramatic."

"A defense lawyer," Bianka decided.

Blue laughed at her. "And sangria when you come back please."

"I expect a good tip." It was a joke now. Blue and the dragons were family now. She raised her voice. "Anything else while I'm out?"

"Marshmallows please," Andre requested.

"Right." Standing on the steps of the brownstone, Bianka realized with a pang that she was going to miss it. The insanity, the laughter, the shopping, Chappy, and even the time-starfish. As she stepped out onto the street, the beat felt different than usual. She frowned. It was the first time that it didn't feel like the backbeat of a dance club under her feet. She looked around the frozen set of people that she'd been passing every day. The homeless men she'd been feeding each had a bag on their arms that she'd placed there to hold the food she was giving them. Who knew, maybe it would give them enough of a start to get back on their feet if they didn't have to worry about eating for a month or two.

There was the large man with the elongated earlobes she thought of as Jumbo. Beyond him was the woman she assumed was a fairy like Blue. Sitting against the wall near the mouth of the alley was the old woman with her walker and a bag of knitting in her lap. Nothing she hadn't seen every day for the past six months. A wave of guilt washed over her. She hadn't heard Serenity's voice in months. Chappy rubbed his head against her chin before he tucked himself into her shirt.

"Shopping," she reminded herself. But she couldn't shake the feeling that something was wrong. Maybe it was just Blue's anticipation of being able to move freely again. She ate like a hummingbird but despite her human appearance, she didn't seem to have the same biological concerns. It was annoying and rather convenient at the same time. Of course, she didn't have to help shovel dragon dung either. "Marshmallows, sangria, meat for the baby, meat for the parents, something tasty for a snack, and scandal magazines."

She found the meat first and hauled it back to the house for Linnaeus to store away. He was as strong in his human form as he was in his dragon form and that Bianka was jealous of the way he could pick up that many pounds while looking like a beanpole. Then, she found the marshmallows and without any guilt at all she added chocolate and graham crackers to the list because she was going to have a dragon toasted marshmallow before this day ended.

Sangria was easy to find, but she wanted a non-alcoholic version to try on Blue as a cut-off and that meant finding a whole pile of fruit juices as well. Still, it was done and all that was left was gossip. She found a stack of what looked like recycling and sorted through it looking for the latest dates. She was near an alley and the questing tendril of a Time-Miester curled over her toe. It darted back immediately. She eyed it, but it didn't creep any closer. It was obviously following her though as she stepped back from the shadows. Closer examination showed that it was probably a baby if they had such things. It was tiny compared to the one she'd pinned to the wall.

A disturbing thought occurred to her. What if they grew new bodies when you cut them apart like some worms? They didn't seem to want to bother with her anymore, but this one was following her with what was either hunger or curiosity. She knelt down and put her hand out. The thin tendril wrapped around her finger, but there was no pain or feeling of danger. It was curiosity and she let it explore her hand. What she could see was no larger than an actual starfish, but with longer black tentacles like an octopus. There were no eyes visible. It pulsed with the same beat as the streets beneath her feet. She stood up with her pile of newspapers and its touch slid off of her fingers.

It followed her back to the brownstone. She sat down on the front steps and the baby Time-Meister crawled up the side of the railing and settled there. She kept an eye on it from the side of her eye, but it didn't seem to want anything more than to sit and observe. Chappy sat on her shoulder and stared at it. "You okay, Chappy?"

//Assent.//

"Is it dangerous?"

//Negative.//

"Okay then." She busied herself looking for more mentions of Pomegranate. The newspapers were no more reliable than a supermarket scandal rag. She frowned at the lead story: Centaur and Dryad Challenge Court Ruling. So there had to be some sort of justice department. She read the article and her gorge rose. She swallowed hard. There wasn't a court system as she was thinking about it. There were courts, royal courts, and they made the decisions. Legal and illegal were simply decisions made by the royal who was asked to mediate the situation. Precedence seemed to exist, but nothing written down. Contracts were sacred it seemed, but they were enforced by some sort of magic, not by a law enforcement team.

She moved through the papers quickly looking for what she really wanted to know, what sort of family had he tried to start. Was having his child enough to mean that she was a "family" member to him? Was she one of the reasons he was in trouble with the Queen he was sworn to? No matter how mad she was at him for walking out, she would never have demanded he stay if it were against his promises. Her father had taught her to keep her promises.

Motion caught her attention and her head snapped to the side. The baby Time-Meister crawled down to the street and into the shadows to hide itself as a much larger creature slide over the walls. She retreated into the house. A baby she might let explore, but an adult whose tentacle was thicker around than her own waist was not getting its tentacles on her.

Chapter 18

The time-bubble shattered with a rush of wind that stole Bianka's breath. She stood for a moment feeling the alpaca strap around her wrist and the pulsing beat of the marketplace throughout her body, not just through her feet. Blue stretched. She stood carefully, but Bianka had to catch her as her knees gave way. "Huh," the fairy said, "that's weird. It's like they just don't remember what to do right now." She stomped her foot on the ground, one hand wrapped around Bianka's arm, the other gripping the side of the chair.

"You've not injured yourself?" Andre asked, concern obvious in her voice.

"No, I'm fine, just need to wake myself up," Blue assured. She toddled a few steps forward and back. The house had not transformed back into a house yet. Or maybe now that they knew it wasn't a house they couldn't see it that way again, either way, the floor was uneven with gold coins and the occasional jewel. A few minutes later and they were ready to leave. Many hugs and kisses for the baby later, Bianka and Blue were in front of the door.

"You have your paper-work?"

Blue patted the bag on her hip. Linnaeus had found it somewhere in a back room and provided it as a thank you gift for Blue blessing their baby. The door opened to a swirl of movement and color and sound. Bianka winced back from it. It was so different from before. Jumbo was gone and the old woman was actually knitting. The homeless guys were pawing through their bags with surprised and happy smiles.

Chappy crawled onto Bianka's shoulder. "Back to the hotel?" Bianka suggested.

Blue nodded. "Yes, I think that's best. I want a nice long bath and a nap. And about three bottles of wine that haven't been watered down."

"Hush. It's better for you."

"Says you."

"Yes, says me."

Blue rolled her eyes and headed for the alleyway. "Come on, let's get back there."

"How about we don't go through the dangerous alley?"

"It's not dangerous. I don't know why you think it is."

The two homeless guys were watching them. The taller of the two caught her eyes and tipped her an imaginary hat. She smiled at them and inclined her head. Blue tugged her toward the alley and they had a quick conference with each other. They hauled their bags up and followed. "We're here, Miss," the one on the left said. His voice was grumbling and low. "Don't you worry."

"I've got it. You two just take care of yourselves."

The one on the right huffed out a laugh. "Miss," his voice was lighter, "we'll follow and make sure you just have to worry about the little one."

Blue looked between them with a little frown. "Bee?"

"I'll explain later. Let's get you home for a bath and some sleep." Blue led them through the alley. Bianka fingered the knife on her hip and her eyes darted through the space. She forced herself to breathe evenly, though all she wanted to do was run. They made it through with nothing attacking them. The boys were still following them. Blue was obviously flagging by the time they got to the gates. The boys stopped there.

"See you tomorrow, Miss," the tallest man waved. Then, they were absorbed into the mass of people leaving the marketplace. The hotel seemed washed out and pastel compared to the vitality of the riot of color they'd left. Blue flopped onto her bed without changing clothes. Bianka laughed at her.

"Do you need help?"

"Just leave me here to die. But bring me chocolate first." Blue muttered into her pillow.

"Do you want a nap before your bath?"

"No, bath. Then sleep. Chocolate first though?"

Bianka made sure Blue was fed. Then, as the fairy's eyes drooped shut, she shepherded her into her bedroom. She helped her get out of the most restrictive pieces of her clothing and then tucked her under the soft blanket. Blue was asleep a breath later. Bianka turned off the lights and poured her a glass of juice for next to her bed in case her blood sugars were too low.

Then, she made her way down to the car. She needed to hear her daughter's voice. "Hello, Seri," she said.

"Hi, Mom! How was the dragon?" she giggled.

"Very nice. And just had a baby. Adorable thing all pink and soft."

Serenity laughed. "When will you be home?"

"In a few days. Have you been keeping up with your worksheets?"

"Yes, Mom. Gramma is making sure I do everything. Can we go to the zoo when you get home?"

"Sure, baby." After the nightmare of the marketplace just worrying about metal contact would be a relief.

"Yeah! She said 'yes'!" Serenity called out not bothering to cover the phone. "Gramma says she wants to talk to you now. I love you."

"I love you too, sweetheart."

"Bee?" her mother queried. "The zoo?"

"Honestly, after a week of negotiations and lawyers, I think it will be relaxing."

Her mother laughed. "And the 'dragon'?"

"Has just had a baby and is ridiculously adorable about it. But I don't have any firm answers. Blue does have the paperwork to get custody of her daughter, but her daughter has to agree to it. We're going to see her husband and daughter tomorrow. Or maybe the day after, depending on how worked-up Blue gets. I think we inadvertently ended up with some bodyguards from a local gang. I happened to give one of the members some chocolate when he was feeling down and now, he seems to think we're his responsibility."

Her mother laughed again. "Only you, Queen Bee. Seri, put that down please."

"Mom, I think we should live together again. All three of us."

"Really? Are you sure?"

"Yes. It's just that it was so difficult getting the apartment set up the way it is, and there's not enough room for all of us. And there's no way I'll be able to afford a house."

"You let me think about things for a little bit, sweetie. We'll figure things out. I don't need much room. We could put two beds in the big bedroom in your apartment."

"I'm usually working at night, so we could use one big bed and just share it?"

"Maybe. I'll start thinking about what I can't leave behind."

"I love you, Mom."

"I love you too, Bianka."

"I have some jewelry that Seri's father left for me. It's silver. Maybe we can get something for it." Bianka stared at the market gate. A small black shadow was moving at the base of it. "Mom, my battery's about to die. I'll call you tomorrow?"

"Be careful, honey."

"I will." They hung up without saying goodbye. Bianka stared at the shadow. It wasn't coming any further across the parking lot as though it had hit a barrier that it couldn't cross. It wasn't the boys. She narrowed her eyes. She was pretty sure that it was a Time-Meister. But they weren't supposed to be visible when time was moving properly.

She plugged her phone in to charge and went into the bedroom to check on Blue. The fairy was asleep, but the juice had been drained. She refilled the glass and left her to sleep. She took a shower and watched blue glitter and street grime swirl down the drain. She was going to have to burn everything she'd brought on this trip. It was all contaminated with glitter.

Chappy sat on the vanity counter and looked at himself in the mirror. He pressed his forelegs against it while Bianca dried off. "You're not fooling me. You're looking at my boobs," she informed him.

//Assent// he agreed happily. He followed her to her room and waited until she had her bra on to settle in his favorite spot. //Hunger//

"Okay. Okay. Let's get you some soda, buddy."

Bianka looked through the fridge and nearly wept in joy when she saw the familiar brands chilling there. She opened a Coke and poured some into a saucer for Chappy. He lapped at it happily and she finished the bottle off herself. Then, she started a pan of mac and cheese.

Blue stumbled out of her room when the food was ready. "Food?" She was bleary eyed and there was a red mark on her cheek from a fold in her pillowcase. Bianka scraped half of the pan onto a plate for her. "Thanks," Blue managed. She ate with her eyes closed. She finished off two sodas, the mac and cheese, and a candy bar before stumbling back to her bed. Bianka wasn't offended. She found the remote and turned on the television to catch up with the news. That didn't hold her interest for more than a minute, so she flipped through the channels until she found what looked to be fairyland's answer to "All My Children" and settled in for some melodrama.

Blue came out a little while later and laid down on the couch next to Bianka. She was only nominally awake. "Remind me to never do that again unless it's an emergency."

"Will do."

The soap operas gave way to news. "Oh, shut that off. It's nothing but gossip and in-fighting. This station is owned by the Fall Queen, so it's biased."

"Do I need to remember any of these political things?"

"No, you're fine."

"Even if my Nate is a Knight?"

"Shit. Did you want to get some sort of money out of him?"

"No, I just want to make sure he can't change his mind and try to take Serenity from me."

"Never happen. Knights aren't allowed to have families without their Royal's permission. He can't even pursue it." Blue yawned. "If you go up two stations, there's a music channel." Bianka obediently changed the channel until Blue fell asleep to the music. Then, she smirked down at the sleeping woman and flipped channels until she found "Cops" and zoned out herself.

Chapter 19

The Market was the usual riot of color. A rainbow of glitter was falling in a waterfall just beyond the gate. Blue shook her head. "Do you want to go back for an umbrella?"

"I don't think it would make any difference. It is going to affect my look a bit though."

Blue snickered. "That's okay, I think everyone understands the intent." Chappy stirred when he saw the glitter and hid himself under Bianka's shirt.

"Let's get going then." The shower of glitter was surprisingly warm. Bianka held her breath as they passed through it. When she looked down at herself her black on black outfit looked like a strange galaxy print. She shook her head like a dog and glitter went flying. Chappy peeked out from his hiding place and promptly sneezed on her. "Wonderful, snot." The hamster-moth didn't bother to reply. He simply looked around and the hid under her now glittery shirt, his usual space as filled with the stuff. "It's going to take years to get this stuff off."

"I recommend fire," Blue told her. She looked like her normal blue-glitter self. There wasn't a hint of any other color on her. She batted her lashes at Bianka's sour look. "I think you look lovely."

"Wench."

Two familiar scarecrow men appeared at their sides. "Morning, Miss."

"Morning, boys," she replied with a smile. "You know, if you're going to keep walking with us, we should probably know your names."

"They call me 'Rocks,'" said the taller of the two.

"And I'm 'Sparky.'"

"Call me 'Bee' and this is Blue."

They nodded. They looked like brothers and Bianka chose to think of them that way. They both had brown hair and dark eyes that could be mistaken for black. They were carrying bags over their backs that looked like they probably carried everything they owned, but they were balanced to fight. "Where we heading, Miss?"

Blue answered, "Court offices for the Summer Court." There was a challenge in the tone as though she expected the location to scare them off.

The two blinked a bit, but then nodded. "Alright then," Rocks said gamely.

Blue led the way through the press of people for once as focused as the executive she was in the outside world. She did stop at a wine shop and defiantly bought herself a glass of spiced wine with a smug look at Bianka. Bianka smiled indulgently, sure that her mixes were better than anything she'd buy at a cheap stand. "So tell me about yourselves," she said to Rocks and Sparky.

"Nothing much to tell, Miss. Me and Sparky are Hellhounds." He shrugged. "We do what needs doing and most folks ignore us."

"Act as bodyguards? Protecting carts? That sort of thing?"

Rocks wrinkled his nose. "Escorting folks places," he agreed finally. "Making sure folks pay up when they're bound to. That sort of thing." He nodded firmly. "Most folks don't care about us much unless they need something."

"You have a safe place to stay at night?"

"No one bothers a Hellhound, Miss," Sparky said. "We work as a pack mostly."

"Oh, there's more in your pack? I'm sorry, I would have..."

"Not anymore, Miss," he interrupted. "Rocks and me are the last of our pack. We ain't found a new one to join yet."

Blue looked over at them. "My condolences," she said.

"Not to worry, Miss Blue. We been scraping by." Rocks' voice was steady, but his eyes were sad. Bianka gave his shoulder a squeeze, then did the same for Sparky. The action left trails of glitter on their shoulders, but they probably wouldn't notice until later.

"It's not the same though."

"No," Sparky agreed. "Can't dwell on it though. Dog'll go mad that way."

"True," Blue agreed. She drained her wineglass and let it drop. It disappeared before it hit the ground, presumably back to the merchant who sold it in the first place. "I'm assuming that Bee is going to make me a better mix of wine later."

"Maybe. If you're nice."

"I'm never nice," Blue lied. "If they're coming with us, they'll need ties."

"Right. I'll keep an eye out for something on the way."

Rocks and Sparky seemed fine walking silently with them and it was calming to have someone at her shoulder. People seemed to move out of their way, but it was probably because there were four of them rather than anything particular about them. They didn't seem to be passing any clothing shops. There weren't any selling scarves either, which was especially odd. Bianka tried not to frown, since that seemed to disconcert people here. Blue bounced from wine shop to wine shop on the way to the court offices. She didn't finish the last glass. "That is just vile," she muttered as she poured it out into a planter in front of the court offices.

The court offices were in a towering, shining, skyscraper. It was ice blue with tiny lights all along the edges. There was a guard at the front door in all black with a crossbow hanging from his hip. They stopped outside the building. Blue removed her end of the belt, so Bianka undid her end and tucked it away in one of the many pockets on her cargo pants. "Okay, let's make ourselves presentable." Bianka fished in her pocket for the roll of black ribbon she'd been given by the old peddler when this all began. There should be enough to create little bowties for her new friends.

Rocks stood with his chin up. Bianka measured out a length of ribbon, cut it with her knife, and tied it around his throat, closing up his shirt with a neat, flat bow. He stood a little taller as she did. He grinned at her. "Thanks, Miss."

Sparky had straightened his shirt and lifted his chin to give her access to his throat. Bianka measured out another length of ribbon and created another bow for him. "Thank you, Miss." He too seemed thrilled by the idea. Their smiles made her smile too. She was surprised but pleased to note that there was still plenty of ribbon available. She put it back into her pocket. She tried to brush off some of the rainbow glitter, but it seemed that would be a lost cause given Blue's giggles.

Bianka shook her head. "Well, I supposed that's the best I can do. Unless you can deal with this, Blue?"

Blue shook her head. "It's not my glitter, so I can't control it."

"Great. Glittered by some over-enthusiastic party-boi." Chappy investigated the bow ties, settling on Sparky's shoulder for a moment. He rested his paws on the ribbon.

//Want//

"Okay, come here." Bianka pulled the ribbon out and created a little tie for Chappy that wouldn't interfere with his wings. "Better?"

//pleasure// He settled onto her shoulder and sat with as much dignity as a moth-hamster could. She noticed the guard's mouth twitch at the look as they passed into the building, but his eyes were kind. He could laugh at her glittered self, she would. The inside of the court building had soaring ceilings and was filled with silvery light and small rainbows that darted from place to place. The furniture on the other hand was ebony dark and seemed to suck in the light.

The reception desk was long and had multiple heights along it. It was designed with more than just humans and wheelchairs in mind. The tallest counters were for something larger than the giant she'd seen in the marketplace. Maybe Andre in her dragon form would use one that height. The smallest counter height was below her knee. Similarly, the counters were operated by a variety of individuals from what she recognized as centaurs to some darkly shrouded form with red eyes.

Blue guided them to the counter with a fairy behind it that was properly sized for humans and fairies. "And how can I help you, Ma'am?"

"I'm here to apply to the Court of Summer for an appointment with Merchant Cornflower and the Queen on the subject of my daughter's custody."

The fairy behind the desk frowned. "And you would be?"

"Periwinkle Jones, the child's mother."

"One moment." The fairy stepped to the back to discuss something with her supervisor. Bianka assumed it had something to do with needing the Queen involved. The two consulted a large book that was summer yellow with little roses around the edge of it. They flipped through a few pages, then found the entry they seemed to be looking for. The discussion continued for a few minutes before the fairy returned.

"Your appointment will be in two hours, if Merchant Cornflower agrees. If not, it will be in two days. We will have an answer run to you if you would like to wait in the cafe. Food and drink in the Court Building are free to all with no obligations. Please eat and drink deeply, there will be nothing asked of you. Please remember that this is a neutral zone and all parties are held to the neutrality contract. No physical altercations unless you are deciding something in one of the official rings. The cafe is within a maintained time orb. The time orb will make your wait no longer than half an hour." With that the fairy handed them what amounted to a pager and sent them in the direction of the cafe.

Chapter 20

The cafe was a coffee-house version of the Star Wars cantina. There were creatures of all shapes and sizes sitting around small tables of varying heights and materials. It looked like it had been decorated by thrifting and craigslist giveaways. The walls were covered with handmade art and lined by cases with pre-packaged foods and drinks. There was a long-suffering barista behind the coffee bar. She was the soft color of an ash tree with leaves twined in her hair and a green apron.

"Hello!" she called out. "Please enter freely and partake freely. This is a neutral place, and all are welcome." It had the ring of ritual more than normal customer service. Bianka nodded a greeting to her. There was a table just in front of the counter that cleared out as they came in. Sparky held Bianka's chair for her and she smiled a gentle thank you. Blue rolled her eyes and went to find herself a small bottle of wine.

"What can I get you, Miss?" Rocks asked.

"Sweet tea if they have it. Otherwise, just some water." Rocks nodded and went in search of drinks while Sparky settled down next to her.

"Miss, what are you doing after this?"

"We'll see how it plays out with Blue. Then, I'll be heading home for a while. I need to see my daughter. And my mother. And get back to work. Some of us can't afford to be off too long."

He nodded. "Me and Rocks used to take care of the kids. You know, before the pack got gone. The kids got taken into other packs, but we were too old."

"That is rough." Bianka shook her head. "I just don't understand people sometimes. It's not like you couldn't take care of yourselves. Or even keep taking care of the kids."

"I love kids," he said wistfully. "They always see things so positive. Not so fond of teething kids, but who is?"

"I remember those days. I do not remember them fondly, but I remember them. At least Seri made it through."

"Sweet tea, Miss." Rocks set down a cup of black coffee for Sparky and a latte for himself. Blue returned with a bottle of red wine and a glass.

"This is actual wine. Not fruit juice," she informed Bianka. "Wine."

"And you would be better off with the fruit juice. Do you really want to be drunk when going into court? What will your ex say?"

"Nothing because he drinks just as much wine as I do." Blue's voice was confident, but her eyes flicked way.

"Really?"

Blue sighed and put the wine back. She returned with a bottle of sparkling grape juice. "I hate you just a little bit right now."

"I haven't even suggested AA."

"I've seen you playing with that keychain of yours."

"Jazz would be more than happy to sponsor you. She's been clean for fifteen years."

Blue considered. "Your girlfriend from the bar? With the pretty scarves and the iron will?"

"That's her."

"Maybe. Oh, did you call her? I think I remember her declaring that she wanted to hear from you every few days."

"My battery died yesterday as I was talking to Mom. I'll call her tonight. I called her when we got here and left a message. She works nights after all."

"Sponsor?" Rocks asked.

"For AA. I'm an alcoholic and an addict and I've been working with Jazz so that I don't go back down that path."

Sparky frowned. "Ok. No alcohol and no drugs." He nodded as though confirming something for himself. "You said work?"

"I'm a bartender." Bianka's smile was more of a smirk as they assimilated that information. Blue rolled her eyes. She was half-way through the bottle of juice already, but that was normal. She was after calories more than flavor. Maybe they could get her onto some sort of protein and fruit shakes. She'd try that when she had access to her favorite blender at work. She didn't have a blender or even a food processor at home. Those had metal blades and she couldn't afford the possibility of contaminated food for Serenity. No, she used a set of ceramic knives she'd found at three in the morning at Walmart when she was desperate for something to take her mind off of the quiet and cold apartment. Serenity had been in the hospital and Nate had left her.

Rocks and Sparky had been having a conversation in glances and gestures and Bianka did them the courtesy of not trying to interfere in it. "Blue?" she queried the fairy. She'd gone quiet and calm.

"I'm scared," she said softly. Bianka reached over and took her hand. "Thank you for staying with me."

"Of course, honey. I'll be here the whole time. I'll call Jazz if I have to. She'll keep taking my hours. And my mom will take care of the bills and things at my place."

Blue took a deep breath. "And if I wanted to get you to work for me?"

"Blue, I will be your friend. I will be your protector, but I will not be your employee anymore. We're family, right?"

Blue nodded a shimmer of glitter flowing from her hair. "Yes, we're family." There were tears shining in her eyes. She took a deep breath and didn't let herself cry. "I don't know why I'm so emotional today."

"This is a big deal. How long has it been since you've seen your daughter?"

"Three years. I don't know how long it's been in the Underhill. I've lost track of the conversion."

"Is there a strict conversion?"

"Not always."

"And has she ever lived in... I guess Overhill? Outside? I don't think Real World counts."

"Overhill works, but mostly we use Outside. She lived Outside with me and her brother until he was killed. Then, it was safer for her to be Underhill. I couldn't protect her." Blue straightened her shoulders. "I can now. But she may not remember Outside."

"How old was she when she went to live with your husband?"

"Five. She should still be five."

"Should be?"

Blue bit her lip. "I lost track of time for a while," she admitted. "It could be longer than three years since I've seen her. It hurt so much when I lost Aster that I got lost for a little while. I buried myself in work and bars. When I surfaced, I had the power to create a safe space for my children. Child."

"And if she says 'no'?"

"She won't."

Bianka didn't push it. She drank her sweet tea and just held Blue's hand. The boys contented themselves with a quick game of cards. It was some game with rules they'd made up, probably when they were kids themselves. The little pager started to glow, and a court page hurried over to their table. He was a teen with fall leaves woven into his hair. "Miss Blue and party? Your court session will start soon. If you'd follow me, please."

They all stood up to follow him and their table cleared itself. The teen took the pager and led them through the corridors and into a back courtyard filled with flowers of all colors. "Through these doors in the Court of Summer. The Court of Autumn will provide the security for this meeting. Merchant Cornflower and Lawyer Scarlet Sage are ready to review the custody request. The Summer Queen is in residence to hear the arguments." The page shifted uneasily. "As this is a family matter, the hearing will be restricted to the parties in the matter."

Bianka narrowed her eyes at him. "Will Blue need her lawyer here as well? If so, we will need someone to run to Andre Draconis."

The page blanched. "Only if she wishes to have him in attendance, ma'am." He bobbed a bow at her.

"Blue?"

"No, I trust in his paperwork." Blue was standing tall, every inch the professional woman she was in the outside world. The door opened and Bianka only got a glance at it before a far too familiar face was blocking her way.

"Family only, ma'am." The knight in front of her was Nate. Her Nate was trying to separate her from Blue and she was not going to let that happen.

"I am here to protect her. Specifically, from her husband. If you do not get out of my way, I will knee you."

"Bee, you wouldn't!" Nate protested. "I'm just doing my job."

"Move. Now."

Beyond them the court page was announcing "Blue Freeman-Time." Blue was startled by that, but Bianka figured that the page only announced nicknames in a place like this. Real names had too much power after all.

"Bee, sweetheart."

Bianka caught him by the back of the neck and kneed him in the stomach. He crumbled. He groaned. The other knights moved toward her, but then hesitated. "You abandoned me and your daughter, you useless bastard. I am not abandoning my responsibilities for you or anyone else." She stepped over him.

She heard Rocks and Sparky snickering behind him. The other knights seemed discomforted, but at her announcement that she had a child with Nate they had faded back and carefully looked elsewhere. The page stumbled only a moment before announcing, "Queen Bee Freeman-Time and attendants." Definitely announcing nicknames. Her mother used to call her Queen Bee. It made sense that a family court would use family nicknames.

The room was a circle with two rows of bench seating in an arc facing the tall throne where the Queen of Summer was seated. She was attended by two knights, one to each side. She was beautiful. Her skin was a healthy dirt brown with chestnut colored eyes. Her hair was a mix of yellow and brown and festooned with a crown of summer flowers that flowed down over themselves at the back. Her dress was a light and airy sunshine yellow with little shimmers of what looked like captured water edging the bottoms of her sleeves. Her throne was a curl of tree roots with flowers and mushrooms growing in the hollows.

Bianka gave her a formal nod before seating herself behind what seemed to be Blue's table. The Queen gave her an amused smile and returned the nod. Rocks and Sparky settled in the row behind her and slightly to each side of her. She assumed they were going to continue their card game. The Queen refocused on the three fairies in front of her. "Begin."

Chapter 21

"As this request comes from Periwinkle, we will ask her to explain why she has called for this meeting," the lawyer said. At least, he looked like a lawyer, with a formal suit and tie that matched the red streaks in his hair. Next to him was Cornflower. His hair had blue streaks like Blue's and all things being normal he could have passed as Blue's brother not her lover.

Blue stood. "I am here to present paperwork to Cornflower and my daughter Gloriosa. If Gloriosa signs this paper, I will be her primary guardian once again. I admit to this court with regret that in my grief and fear, I allowed Cornflower to be the sole parent for Gloriosa. However, coming back to my senses, I have felt a hole in my heart, and I need to be reunited with the child I left Underhill for her own protection."

"I will review the papers," Scarlet Sage stated. Blue relinquished them for him to read and the Queen studied Blue.

"Periwinkle Jones, it has come to our attention that you yourself have recently been adopted. Does your new clan also consider itself matrilineal?"

Blue glanced over her shoulder with a half-smile. "My new mother has a mother and a daughter, but no husband and no father. She is the head of her household and her biological daughter is her heir."

The Queen nodded slowly. Her eyes lifted and fixed on Bianka. Bianka lifted her chin and met the gaze evenly, ignoring the glitter, ignoring the whispers of the guards at the door. "Queen Bee, you sit before us as a mother only?"

"I am mother and protector for Periwinkle," she confirmed. "I refused to be separated from her and I promised to protect her and support her during her custody negotiations." A mother's protection had kept them safe in the marketplace, hopefully that was work here as well.

"Then welcome, mother of Blue Freeman-Time, we are pleased that our former child has found a protector in the Outside World who will support and keep her safe. Though we regret the need for such actions."

Bianka bowed her head. "Thank you for trusting me with her," she responded.

"These papers refer to Periwinkle Jones, not Blue Freeman-Time," Scarlet argued. "Who she once was is not who she is now. These papers are not valid."

"She is and will always be Periwinkle Jones. She is just also Blue Freeman-Time," Bianka snapped, not allowing Blue to say a word. Blue looked over her shoulder, eyes wide. Crap, what was the proper protocol for this. She didn't know and they didn't have a lawyer here. "If we need to, we can call Lawyer Andre Draconis to explain the paperwork."

Scarlet Sage paled a bit at that. "That won't be necessary, ma'am, er, your majesty?"

The Queen of Summer narrowed her eyes. "We recognize our child Periwinkle Jones, no matter what new name she uses now, and suggest that in bringing this to the Court of Summer, it is proper that she should use the name she has always held in Summer. Are there other arguments against this contract?"

"Periwinkle has not had any contact with the child since she was moved to the Underhill by her father," Cornflower stated, not looking at anyone but the queen. "She also has not applied directly to me to visit with the child since she left her in my care. So, I question why suddenly she seems to worry about her."

"I have always cared about Gloriosa. After her brother was stolen by a bullet, I realized that I could not protect her in the Outside. It was for her own safety that I agreed to let her live with Cornflower here while I tended to our business in the Outside. My financial support has never wavered."

"Financial support is no substitute for actual maternal care," Scarlet interrupted his client before he could say something else.

Blue wavered a bit but steadied her shoulders. "I will admit that I have made mistakes, but I am here today to rectify those mistakes. The paperwork that Lawyer Scarlet Sage holds is only valid should Gloriosa herself agree to it. I am here before you, your majesty, to request the opportunity to present the contract to her without her father's interference."

"I protest, I would never interfere in Periwinkle's contact with her daughter, if she had ever requested it."

"If Cornflower had responded to the past five missives sent to him, I would not be here today, your majesty." Blue pulled a small booklet out of her bag. "These are copies of the formal correspondence between the two of us, with records of when they were sent and that they were received by Merchant Cornflower's staff."

"Time runs differently here and out there," Cornflower said snidely. "In case you don't remember. All of this correspondence is recent. I haven't had a chance to get back to it."

"And what is the age of the child?" the queen asked.

"Eight, your majesty. She's lived with me since she was five and has not seen her mother since that time."

"That would be nearly fifteen years Outside," she stated. "We will review the correspondence." One of the queen's knights stepped forward to receive the papers. "What other arguments do you have which would prevent a mother from seeing her daughter?"

"Periwinkle is a drunk," Cornflower stated. He still hadn't bothered to look at Blue and Bianka wondered how much of that was anger and stung pride and how much of it was betrayal. Blue shook her head.

"For a year Outside, I did not handle my grief well and hid in a bottle. However, my drinking has not affected my ability to run a business, tend to myself, or maintain a home. After those months of grief, however, I received no answers from Merchant Cornflower. I pursued the recommended paths and received no answer. It came to the point where I felt it necessary to find a protector and seek the advice of Lawyer Draconis."

"She's still a drunk. Always was and always will be. And I wouldn't be surprised if she's been opening her petals for someone else as well."

Jealousy and pride, Bianka decided. He was a bitter ex-boyfriend who wasn't even an ex. Although, she was willing to bet that dissolution of the marriage wouldn't be too hard, given the interaction in front of her today. She glared at the back of Cornflower's head. She couldn't disagree that Blue's previous behavior with wine was a bad example, but she had actually put the wine back and gone for a non-alcoholic drink in the cafe. If this fell through, and if Blue really was considered her daughter here, maybe she could get her into some sort of fairyland rehab or AA program.

"Mother Bee, would you attend us please?" the Queen of Summer asked gesturing her to come forward.

"Of course." She approached the throne and mounted the steps as the queen gestured her closer. Rocks and Sparky shifted uneasily on the chair but didn't rise to accompany her.

"Would you say that Blue's drinking is problematic?"

"I think it was problematic, but we spent time in one of her time-bubbles weaning her off of pure wine all the time. She's down to a few glasses a day from the bottles she was drinking. But if I have my way, I will get her a sponsor and have her going to meetings in the Outside. I've been in recovery myself for several years and I do think she needs support. However, that said, I also think that she's financially and emotionally available to support her daughter. I think her willingness to face her fears and to deal with Andre shows her commitment to doing just that."

The Queen of Summer nodded. "Thank you for your council, Queen Bee. And for your honesty. We do not hear much of that." The woman pointed with her chin at the lawyer and his client who were quietly discussing something at their table. "And your Xeitus is adorable."

"This is Chappy," she introduced. "He wanted a bow tie, so he'd match the boys." She gestured absently at Rocks and Sparky.

"It does suit." The queen smiled. "I will have a page give you an address for Outside by which you can always reach me. I would like updates on Blue's progress."

"I will keep her secrets, but I can provide a general update, sure."

"Thank you."

Bianka might not have been a courtier, but she understood the end of conversation when she heard it. She nodded and returned to her seat, though she paused to give Blue's shoulder a squeeze. The queen took her time reading through the papers Blue had provided to her.

"Merchant Cornflower, Merchant Periwinkle, it is our decision that the child will be given the opportunity to talk with her mother unsupervised by this court or by her father. However, in the interests of safety, Lawyer Scarlet Sage and Queen Bee will oversee the discussion though they will not be able to interfere."

Chapter 22

The room Scarlet Sage, Bianka, and Blue were led to was white, with a metal table bolted to the floor and metal chairs to sit on. "Oh, Hell no," Bianka said grabbing the arm of the bailiff. He looked at her with a wide-eyed sort of terror. He was too young for this job. "This is not a room where you meet a child. This is a room where you say goodbye to your father because he just got twenty to life. The family meeting room should have a carpet, some chairs, a box of tissues at least?" She raised her brows at him meaningfully. It should look something like the hospital's grief counselor's office.

The room in front of them started to change. There was a carpet on the floor covered in autumn leaves and four chairs of twisted wood took over for the table. A small round side-table with a box of linen handkerchiefs popped into existence. The walls were a warm orange shade. Bianka refused to let the magic throw her. "Much better," she said to the young fairy. Blue had told her that "thank you" was a bad idea for this world. It led to complications they didn't need. She released his arm and smiled at him.

"Of course, ma'am. I'll just let you wait until Merchant Cornflower brings his daughter."

"And there is a guard with the daughter to make sure that he's not prompting her to automatically say 'no' to anything her mother asks?"

Scarlet Sage cleared his throat. "There is a geas on him to not poison testimony of anyone involved until the resolution of the matter," he said. He shifted a bit nervously. She narrowed her eyes at him. Blue hovered near Bianka's side, finger picking at the seam of her new bag and foot tapping.

"The interrogation room was your idea?"

He grimaced a bit. "It's a standard room for client meetings."

"If your clients are families then you are doing them a grave injustice. You made the room terrifying for a small child and set it up so there were two sides as opposed to an open meeting space. If your clients are adults facing jail time for their actions, it might be justified." She waited for him to respond to that.

"Oh look, they've provided some lemonade. Shall we sit?"

"That depends on whether that lemonade is free and clear like the juice in the cafe."

He scowled at her. Blue smirked at them both. The lemonade disappeared. "I see why you didn't bring a lawyer."

Blue laughed. "She's amazing, isn't she?"

Bianka smiled mirthlessly. She settled on one of the chairs. Scarlet Sage took the chair across from her while Blue paced through the room. "Tell me about yourself, Scarlet Sage," Bianka said. "Have you been a lawyer long?"

"Oh, centuries." He waved an elegant hand. "My father was a lawyer as well. It runs in the family." He studied her. "And you? How did you get to adopt Periwinkle?"

"She wanted to come to get her daughter. Now that she's in a position to take care of her again." As if Bianka was going to give him a full answer. "She wanted protection from the Market when she went to see her lawyer. Do you have a specialty? Family law? Corporate?"

"I represent Merchants." He paused. "Your daughter is a merchant as well. I would have assumed that she would have come to our firm before pursuing this action."

"Conflict of interest isn't it? To represent two sides at one time?" Bianka looked over at Blue who was chewing on her nail. "Come and sit down, sweetie," she said. Blue jumped a bit and blinked. She came toward the chair but stopped and shook her head.

"I'm too hyper right now." She wandered around the room once more. Scarlet Sage's eyes followed her with something like concern in them.

"It's common practice. Lawyers are neutral."

"That's pointless. Shouldn't you care about the cases you take?"

He studied her. "That would mean involving ourselves in court politics and that would be foolish. We remain neutral and can represent our clients in any court."

"But you want to win."

"We want the best outcome," he moderated. Bianka gave him her best "mom" look and he shrugged at her. "I want to win," he admitted, "but not at the expense of a child. It's hard enough to get a child in the first place. To get permission to have three? Cornflower and Periwinkle must be favored."

"You haven't worked for Cornflower before?"

Scarlet Sage shook his head. "No."

The door cracked open and Cornflower stepped in. He was scowling, but he sighed. "Gloriosa, your mother is going to talk to you for a little while." He knelt down. "The lady there is your grandmother. If you don't want to talk to Mother any more, tell her that you want to leave, and she'll come get me."

The little girl was tiny. She had wide blue eyes that were surrounded by a simple frame of white glitter. Her hair was tied up into a complex tangle of braids with flowers woven in. She was wearing a simple dress of blue and there was a bracelet on her wrist that looked like actual captured water. She bit her lip. "Mama?" she queried in a shaky voice.

Blue knelt down and opened her arms to her. "Oh, Glori." The little girl stepped carefully across the floor as though she were afraid of stumbling. It made Bianka ache a little bit. She let her mother envelope her in a hug. Blue pressed a kiss to the top of her head and held her tightly for a long moment. Cornflower stepped back as a guard tugged on his arm. The door shut behind him. Leaving the four of them alone.

Gloriosa whispered again, "Mama." Then, her little fingers clenched tightly into her mother's clothing. She sobbed. "Daddy said you were gone forever. That you would never come back for me. That the Outside ate you!"

"No, sweetie. No. I had to stay to keep the business running. Daddy and I have always kept the business in both worlds. You remember that I used to have to go to work. You and Aster used to come with me?"

The little girl shivered. "The Outside ate Aster."

Blue sniffled a little bit. "It's okay to miss him."

"The bad metal killed him. There's no bad metal here."

"The bullet," Blue corrected softly. "You remember the shooting?"

Gloriosa nodded. Her mother lifted her up and carried her over to a chair. She sat the little girl on her lap and started a bubble in what seemed to be an automatic reaction to a crying child. Scarlet Sage cleared his throat before the bubble swept across the room. Blue nodded without saying anything but let the spell fall. She let Gloriosa sob into her shoulder for a long time. She rocked her carefully. Like she was made of crystal. Eventually, the little girl wound down. "Are you coming home, Mama?"

Blue took a deep breath. "I can't let down the people who rely on us Outside," she said finally. "Would you like to come and live with Mama?"

"Outside? With the bad metal?" Gloriosa started to hyperventilate. "Where the bad men will take me away for ever and ever?"

"The bad men will not take you away. You will be safe. The house is very secure. And you and Daddy can visit every weekend. Would you like that?"

Gloriosa's blue eyes were filled with tears. She looked at her mother, but her breathing didn't calm down. She was terrified. She was shaking her head. "Outside is bad."

Scarlet Sage's smile was triumphant, but Bianka couldn't let that stand. "Gloriosa," she said calmly, "take a breath with me. Breathe in and hold it. Two. Three. Let it out." The little girl looked at her but followed the instructions. She obviously had a teacher or a nanny who used the same tone of voice with her. Bianka let her through two more deep breaths. "Better?"

"Yes. Thank you, Ma'am."

"You're scared of Outside?" Blue took her cue from Bianka's voice as well. She rubbed Gloriosa's back. "I guess you don't remember the park? Or the horses?"

"H-horses. Yes, I remember the horses."

"Do you remember the bed with the blue canopy?"

"Purple," she corrected. "And Mr. Teddy. Is Mr. Teddy still on my bed? I forgot to bring him with me."

"Yes, he is." It took a few more minutes of memories for the panic to completely leave her body. "Gloriosa, I have a piece of paper here that means you can come live with me all the time. Would you like that?"

She shook her head. "I don't want to live Outside. I want you to come home and live with me and Daddy."

Blue sagged a bit. "Oh, sweetie. Daddy and I are having disagreements right now." She considered for a long moment. "Maybe you could come and visit me and see if you like it? You could meet Serenity. She's Queen Bee's daughter and she's your age. She's allergic to metal so there's no bad metal in their home."

The little girl considered. "Can we play dress up?" she asked her mother. Blue shot Bianka a questioning glance.

Bianka nodded. Dress up was one of the safest games that Serenity could play. They found most of it at the thrift store or got it as presents from the other families in the apartment building. They had adopted Serenity as soon as they realized that she was sickly. And that Bianka wasn't alone taking care of her. "Will that suit your client?"

Scarlet Sage considered. "I believe it will. He will retain custody, but visitation with her mother for a few days would not be a bad idea. But not today. She's obviously upset."

Blue glared at him. "That should be a discussion we have with Cornflower."

"She has lessons for two more days."

"Then I will expect to see her in two days. Will it be you or Cornflower who brings her to the house?"

"Merchant Cornflower, of course."

"And will this be recorded as a new arrangement by the court? That I have weekend custody?" Blue asked. "And how is time to be measured? By here or there?"

"By here, of course. This is the true time."

Blue's smile was cold. "Cornflower has trouble with the conversion between Outside and Underhill. As do I, is there someone who can hold us to a proper schedule?"

Scarlet Sage was calm for a moment. "I believe so. I would have to consult the court of course. And we need to write up a new contract. Why don't you tear up the other one?"

Blue laughed at him. "No. Gloriosa," she said calmly, "I have a contract that means you could come live with me always. I'm going to keep it and if you ever decide that you want to live with me instead of Daddy, you can sign it and then you'll live with me forever."

"Promise?"
"I promise, honey. I promise."

Chapter 23

Blue was trembling a little bit by the time they got back to the hotel. Bianka bundled her up onto the couch in a throw and handed her a soda. "Get on the outside of the soda and we'll discuss whether or not you are justified in kidnapping your own child for a week rather than a weekend. At least, I think that's what the conversion is."

"I... something like that? I think? Ten days for two." Blue chugged the Coke. "I wasn't going to just keep her. That's why I thought about having someone outside keep track of things. Oh, gods, I have so much to do now. I have to get ready."

"You have two weeks. Do you still have her bed?"

"I moved her bedroom so that it would look just like it did when she was last with me. I kept Aster's too. I just... I couldn't get rid of his things."

Bianka bit her tongue. She wasn't going to criticize her for mourning. Her mother still had her father's things in the house. They were all packed up, but they were there, hiding to ambush them during the holidays, or late at night when they needed another blanket. She sat down next to her, a puff of glitter freeing itself from the crease in her pants. Chappy had found himself a piece of hard candy and was either making out with it or lapping at it. Bianka didn't want to know. Blue scrubbed at her face with a hand.

"Did I do too badly with her?"

"No, but I think she needs a counselor as soon as you get her on a regular schedule."

Blue blinked. "A counselor? A human counselor? Why would I do that?"

"She has panic attacks thinking about her brother's death. She needs to talk to someone. And she's young enough that they'll consider her talking about being Outside as a metaphor. The hospital forced me to talk to a grief counselor when we... I thought we were going to lose Serenity. Nate had bunked on me while I was in the hospital holding her hand. I was a mess for a week. Jazz managed to keep me from drinking or doing something I'd regret, but it was hard. And I had never thought about how much metal there is in everything. I think Dr. Marx thought I might be suicidal. But it helped. It helped a lot."

Blue nodded. "I think maybe we can go together. I would try to get her father to go, but that will not happen."

"Are the two of you still married?"

"We are. Why?"

"Do you actually want to be?"

Blue looked at her and blinked. "Divorce is not an option," she said finally. "The queen would never stand for it. Especially not since we have a child from the marriage still living."

"Even if he were abusive? Or you were? That's ridiculous."

"We don't have to live together, but if we got a divorce, Gloriosa would be considered an Unwanted and we'd have to give her away." Blue's fingers were white around her soda bottle.

"Are there any protections for married partners?"

"Magic in our vows. We cannot physically harm each other or force each other to do anything... you know." Her cheeks flushed. "That was never a problem. I think he's just mad at me."

Bianka bit back her immediate reaction. "I want you to see someone too. I think you need to talk to someone about losing Aster."

Blue closed her eyes. "I don't like talking about it. Telling you was the first time I'd talked about him in years."

"Then it's time to talk to someone. It's been fifteen years according to what you told me at the court. And if it's this painful, then maybe there's something to help you that's not in a bottle."

"Are you really going to be a hard-ass about me drinking? When I'm in the middle of a custody case?"

"Sweetheart, this custody case will be around until your daughter is legal. And that's going to be awhile if you're living Outside and she's living with her father." She pushed a hand through her hair and let herself sigh. "Blue, I'll support your decisions because you are an adult, but I will tell you the truth. I will always tell you the truth because I learned not to lie to myself when I got clean. And it is better to be sober when dealing with bureaucracy or lawyers."

"Why must you be so logical?" Blue pulled the blanket over her face.

"Or I could just remind you about dragon sex."

"Ew." Blue scowled over the edge of the blanket at her. "You are an evil woman and I don't know why I have let you adopt me. It's legally recognized by the way, if you didn't catch that. The Queen of Summer herself recognized it. And she let you act as my mother. That's a big deal."

"So, you'll get the couch when you come to visit. My mother and I are sharing the main bedroom. Probably. If we actually move in together. It will make rent easier to meet every month."

Blue studied her. "You're planning for me? What about the boys?"

"I don't know if I can convince my mother to let two strays live in the apartment with my seven-year-old. I think she'll take exception to it."

"Rocks and Sparky would be great with your daughter. Hellhounds always love kids."

"That's what would concern my mother. That they were loving my daughter without being trusted adults." Bianka shook her head. "It doesn't matter now. Right now, I think you need some food and I need some coffee."

"How about a glass of wine with that food?" Blue asked.

"If your legs are broken, not a chance. But if you are pouring it for yourself, I will not stop you."

Blue flipped the blanket off and practically levitated to the kitchen. Bianka laughed at her and Chappy looked up from his hard candy. He shook his furry rear and settled back down with the candy, opening up his wings. "No comments from the peanut gallery," Blue told the pink hamster-moth. She poured herself a glass of wine and took a big swig. She swallowed and coughed. "Wow, you have seriously been watering down my wine haven't you?"

"Half fruit-juice at least."

"Wench." Blue looked at the cabernet. "Okay, show me the formula because this is really dry."

Bianka pushed herself to her feet and went to the kitchen. "So what's the plan now?"

"We go back to the outside world. I drop you off at the bar and give you a wonderful infusion of cash. Then, I prep for my little girl to come home and come drink at your bar every night." Blue was twitchy. "And we set up a play date for our little girls at my place because it's just as metal free as I can make it. And I will pick you up because I have the distinct impression that you don't drive."

"I don't have a car. I have a license, but not a car. I haven't been behind the wheel in years. I should probably make sure I still remember how."

Blue nodded. "I'll make sure you have access to a ride if you ever need it because that's what daughters do for their mothers."

"We are about to find out if you're ticklish, young lady."

Blue batted her lashes. Bianka poked her in the side. "Don't make me spill the wine."

Chapter 24

Bianka had seen Sparky and Rocks loitering near the entrance to the Market as she and Blue were packing the car, but by the time they were ready to actually leave, they were gone. It was too bad. She'd wanted to say goodbye to them and thank them for their company at the trial. She'd told Chappy that he was free to go whenever he wanted, but he simply snuggled into the side of her neck and sat there radiating smugness. She'd figure out what to do about having a weird pet sometime later. At least he was easy to feed.

As they were dumped back out onto the highway, everything seemed dull and washed out like a faded watercolor. Bianka closed her eyes but couldn't seem to fall asleep. Blue put on her music mix and started singing along with the songs she could at top voice. She was as out of tune as Wenceslas and the Monsters got when there was a particularly obnoxious hipster crowd in the bar. Bianka didn't wince, but it was a close thing. She did not try singing along with the music. Her singing voice was good enough for group hymns at church with her mother when she was a kid, but not good enough that she would every let someone hear her singing on her own.

The rural area slowly turned back to suburban and then they were in the city. Nothing seemed to have changed. The tags on the walls looked the same as always and the cars were just as backed up and full of campaign stickers as usual. "Hey, can we hit the drug store? I need to get the paper."

"Sure." Blue found the closest shop and waited in the car. Bianka nearly coughed at the price of the paper. She normally didn't bother buying it on the day, but she needed the reminder of what was actually happening in the real world. There were three people in line in front of her. The one right in front of her was a tall, thin, and artificially pale Goth with artfully tousled hair that probably wouldn't move if a gale force wind hit it. He gave her a friendly smile that she returned automatically.

With a theatrical bow he said, "Please, go ahead, ma'am."

"It's fine."

"Please. I insist."

Bianka gave him a nod and stepped in front of him. He pulled out his phone and started texting someone. She scanned the front page as she waited. It seemed wrong that the same scandals were on the page. She felt years older, though the paper assured her she'd only been gone six days. She double-checked the year — there were stories about Fairylands. No, only six days missing in the outside world. That meant she could take Seri to the park and have a talk with her mom before she decided to find her way back to the Market and find someone who could get the cure for her daughter. Andre had assured her that the cure could be found for a price. That was more than any normal doctor had managed.

Blue pulled to a stop next to the bar. "Here, this is for the last six months." Blue held out an envelope of cash. It was far too thick for comfort.

"No, that's far too much. I can't."

"Take it." Blue narrowed her eyes. "I will stay right here and stare at the bar. I will follow you back to your apartment. I will lurk on your stairs and wait until the lights go out, then sneak into your house and slip it into your pants."

"That is creepy, and you should be ashamed of yourself."

"You're my mom now, so you only have yourself to blame. Besides, we only negotiated for one week and it's been months, so..." Blue shrugged.

They stared at each other for a moment. Eventually, slowly, Bianka took the thick envelope. She tucked it into her backpack. "Thank you," she said quietly.

"I'll see you around. You can't get rid of me now. We're family." Blue honked twice before she pulled away from the curb.

Bianka poked her head inside to see if Jazz was there working on set-up. She was only slightly disappointed to see that it was Salem. Salem was quiet and didn't tend to talk to anyone when he wasn't actively on shift. She waved at him. He gave her a small smile and raised the bottle he was opening in salute. Bianka closed the door. She shouldered her bag and started walking home.

After months of walking in streets that changed daily, it was nice to know that her way home was the same as it always was. She saw a couple stray dogs which usually only came out during the evening, but they were just in the shadow of the alley. She had always wanted a dog for Serenity, but they just couldn't afford to feed one. Not even with the envelope of cash that Blue had handed her.

"Hey, baby, looking good," one of the idiots lounging on the stairs called.

She ignored him, focused on seeing her daughter's face. Most of the boys in the area knew better than to confront her. She heard a little bit of a scuffle to her side and did her best to evaluate it from the corner of her eye. One of the older boys had smacked the catcaller. "Sorry, ma'am!" he called out to her as he smacked the younger boy again. "Do you have any idea what Mama will do to you if you bother Miss B?" she heard over her shoulder.

Soon enough she was at her mother's apartment. She took a breath before opening the door and did a mental check of what she was wearing – nothing metal on her pants or shirt. No glitter. Everything which had been glittered she'd left in the trunk of Blue's car. "Hey, I'm home," she said as the door closed behind her. She dropped her bag on the floor. A daughter-shaped missile hit her in the stomach with a hug.

"Mommy!!" She found herself wrapping around Serenity with something like desperation. Her hair was in two puff-balls on the sides of her head. They were held with red ribbons that matched the ribbons on the shoulders of her sundress. "You were gone forever!"

"It felt like it. I missed you every day, sweetheart."

"Hello, honey. Have you eaten yet?"

"I wouldn't say no to food." Bianka didn't want to let go of Serenity. She remembered a piece of advice from a Disney actress on hugging kids – never let go until the kid does, so she didn't. Serenity pulled on her hand to drag her to the coffee table where she was working on her homework.

"I got a new science book."

"Oh? Have you finished the other one already?"

"Yep. And I got all the questions right on my quizzes."

"That's wonderful."

"I've got PBJs in the kitchen," her mother said, "but no one eats anything until they wash their hands." Serenity bopped off to the bathroom and its rubber covered faucets. Her mother's apartment had a lot more metal than she really liked Serenity being around. Bianka washed her hands in the kitchen sink. She dried them on the soft kitchen towel. There was a stack of boxes next to the door.

"What're those?" she asked.

"Your father's clothes. I've got one of the boys from the church coming to pick them up for the shelter."

Bianka's head snapped around to see her mother's face. "Mom?"

"It's time. And if we're moving to your apartment, it's just a waste to carry it with us." Her mother's face was serene, but there was a tightness around her eyes. Bianka hugged her carefully, as though she were made of the finest spun sugar. Her mother's arms came up around her tightening until they were as close as they could be. "It's time." Bianka could hear the tears that her mother wasn't crying.

"You don't have to do this if it hurts you."

"It's my decision. I kept the jacket from the wedding and the sweater-vest he used to wear when we went calling." Her mother pulled back from the embrace. "Now, it's time to sit down and eat."

The PBJ's were familiar and simple and made more delicious because Seri was catching her up on everything that had happened while Bianka was away. "And you said we could go to the zoo!"

"I did," Bianka confirmed. "Now, what do we remember about the zoo?"

"There's lots of metal and I have to wear my gloves and a long-sleeved shirt."

"And?"

"And no running away from you because I might get lost and that would scare you."

"Right. So, we'll go tomorrow so we can have the whole day there. Is there anything in your science book that we should take care of while we're there?"

Serenity's face lit up. "I'll go check." She squirmed away from the table without touching the edge. The old metal edge had been wrapped and rewrapped in duct tape for years before Serenity even existed. It was probably time for the poor thing to end up in a dumpster, but it still served as the main eating table, sewing table, laundry table, and everything in between table. It didn't list, thanks to the shims her father had added to the bottom of the leg. Bianka ran a hand over the scuffed Formica.

"I've called and talked to the management office. I think they're glad to see the back end of me. She said that I don't have to finish out next month. She'll pro-rate the rent to the middle of the month to give me time to leave." Dorthea's voice was dry. She shook her head. "Just because I've been here almost twenty years. You'd think that they hadn't been raising the rent on me every year."

Bianka snorted. "Has the rent ever not risen?" Serenity was busy flipping through her science book, so Bianka pulled the envelope out. "This is what Blue paid me for this trip. I think we can use it to pay off the rent for the next month and maybe hire a truck for the move."

"Now Queen Bee, you stop it. You use that money to take care of Serenity and yourself."

"I am. Having you with us is helping us."

Her mother smiled and shook her head. "Bianka Freeman you take care of you and Serenity. Let me worry about me."

Bianka recognized the look in her mother's eyes and backed down. She hadn't actually counted the money in the envelope yet. She thumbed through the stack. Instead of the twenties she assumed it was filled with hundreds. She was going to kill Blue when she saw her next. Although, it might pay for the next meeting with Serenity's doctor. She placed one of the hundred-dollar bills onto the table. "Please take this," she said quietly. "I couldn't have taken this job without your support."

Serenity was back with her science workbook before her mother could deny that. Bianka picked her up onto her knee and they looked over the animal lessons and carefully marked the pages they would work through when they got back from the zoo.

Chapter 25

The apartment seemed too quiet when Serenity went to report her week to her stuffed animals. Chappy stretched his wings and flew around the main room. Serenity hadn't noticed his presence yet and Bianka still hadn't figured out what to do when she did. The apartment had two bedrooms. She'd managed to maintain it through strength of good tips on Saturday nights and the judicious application of charity grants from the medical community. Nate had been with her when they'd rented it. It stung to realize that she'd never have had the credit to get approved for the place without him.

Over the years she'd made it as safe for Serenity as possible. The faucets were covered with plastic and electrical tape. The furniture was all either plastic or old wood furniture she'd found at thrift stores. She'd still had the jewelry that Nate had left for Serenity to sell off. The money that Blue had just handed her would pay for the rent for the rest of the year and that was what she was going to do with it. She stored the envelope away in the empty canister that claimed it was for flour on the front and lived on top of the refrigerator. A few coins rattled around in the bottom. They were a legacy from when she'd hastily cleaned out a pocket of coins so that toddler-aged Serenity wouldn't put them into her mouth.

"Seri, it's time to get ready for bed." Bianka washed her hands. Chappy had found a perch in an awkward corner of the kitchen and was watching her with little black eyes. He fussed with his bowtie a little bit.

"But, Mom, I haven't seen you in forever."

"I'll be in shortly."

She heard water in the bathroom. "Chappy, can you get me back to the Market?"

The hamster-moth didn't respond right away. Eventually, he flew down and curled against her neck. //Query?//

"I need to find out if I can get Seri free of her metal allergy."

//Assent.// He replied. //Soon?//

"It's far away," she warned.

//Negative.//

"There's another way in?"

//Assent. Easy.//

"We'll go after work then. In two days. Let's get you some juice." She poured out a saucer full of juice and set it on top of the fridge.

"Mom? Is that a moth?" Serenity was on her tiptoes trying to see the top of the fridge.

"I'm not sure what he is, but he's friendly." She held Chappy out on her hand and he preened as Serenity very carefully stroked down his back.

"She's so soft."

"He."

Serenity's eyes narrowed. "Did you check?"

"Yes."

//Amusement.//

"Will he be staying with us?" Serenity's voice was full of hope.

"As long as he wants to."

Her face broke into a bright smile and she bounced in place. "We have a pet!"

"As long as he wants to stay. He's still a wild creature. And I don't know how long he'll want to stay cooped up in the apartment. But he seems to really like juice and sweets, so I think we can take care of him. Now, he might not like a lot of people trying to touch him," she warned. "So, we shouldn't tell a lot of people about him."

"Not even Cynthia?"

"Cynthia might feel bad because she can't have pets."

Serenity considered that. "Granma says she might come live with us." She stroked another finger down his back.

"We're talking about it and I think she's going to say yes. She was giving grand-dad's clothes to the church."

"If Granma moves here, do I have to go to church with her?"

"We'll figure that out when the time comes. But there's a lot of metal at the church, so probably not." Bianka had given up on church years ago. Even the thought of losing Serenity hadn't driven her back into it. Her mother, on the other hand, was a long-standing member of the Baptist church. "It will be your decision though. We can do as much as possible to keep you safe, if you want to go."

Serenity focused fully on Chappy and rubbed the top of his head with one finger. "I don't like it there. There's so many people. And they're all so loud and want to touch me."

Alarm bells went off in the back of Bianka's head. Was it agoraphobia or was something happening at the church that she needed to investigate? "We'll talk about it. Now, let's let Chappy eat something. Did you brush your teeth?"

"Yes."

"Wash your face?"

"Yes."

"Okay, get your nightshirt on." She escorted her daughter to her room. When her mother moved in, they could share the bedroom. Bianka could have it in the day and her mother could sleep overnight. Serenity's bedroom was like a small contained explosion of scarves and fabric. She tucked her daughter into the twin bed she'd cobbled together with wood, glue, and a neighbor's husband who happened to know old-fashioned joinery. It was just a box with some slats that held up the mattress. There wasn't a single nail in it.

The quilt that she was snuggled under was hand-made by a local quilting club. She still wasn't sure who had told them about Serenity being in the hospital. Bianka had slept under that quilt in a hard-plastic chair every night she could. Work had kept her sane and she ended up napping fitfully during the day and dragging herself to the bar right from the hospital. She was just lucky enough that Jim was flexible. She still owed him about six hundred dollars from cab fare loans, but he refused to take the money. She sat with Serenity until she fell asleep.

She quietly picked up the scarves and rolled them into little balls and put them back into the cardboard treasure chest that acted as a theatre trunk. She filled the trunk with scarves and skirts and plastic beads. She fussed around the room, picking up discarded ribbons and toys and putting them into place. Serenity was a hard sleeper. She'd learned to sleep through medical procedures as a child, so hearing her mother in the room was nothing.

Chappy settled on her shoulder as soon as she left the bedroom. "I'll be going to bed soon," she informed him. He simply rode around on her shoulder as she cleaned up the house until it was time for her to sleep. She changed into a simple shirt and shorts. She collapsed on the bed and stared up at the ceiling. Laying here, she could pretend that the past few months had never happened. She'd just accompanied Blue to her lawyer and come back home. Then, there was a flying pink-moth-hamster attempting to land on her face. "Are you going to sleep on my pillow, or do you want me to set something up for you?"

Chappy walked across her face and settled on the pillow next to her head.

"Do not walk on my mother when she's here. She'll think you're a rat and try to kill you."

//Amusement. Sleepy.//

"Goodnight, Chappy." Bianka closed her eyes. She was going to the zoo in the morning and then to find a cure for her daughter.

Chapter 26

The sun was shining brightly overhead as they entered the zoo. Serenity was practically skipping alongside them, but she wasn't running off. She had a light, long-sleeved shirt on and white gloves that she'd chosen for the day. She had a surgical mask around her neck in case she wanted to get close to something rusty. Metal particles weren't usually air-borne and there shouldn't be glitter here, so she should be safe without it. It was more of a signal to other people that she was ill. That normally made them give her a little space.

The prairie dogs were the first exhibit. One of them was standing guard and stared at Serenity. She had stopped two steps away from the metal wiring that surrounded the critters. The prairie dog, looking like a groundhog who'd gone on a crash diet, let out a squeak and several of the other ones froze. Bianka stood behind her daughter and watched as the dogs evaluated them and then went back to their usual activities. "Can we take one home?" Serenity asked.

"No, sweetheart. They need to stay with their families. Though they are adorable."

Bianka's mother looked thoughtful. Bianka mouthed "no," at her and was distinctly ignored. There was probably another stuffed animal coming home with them. There was a birthday party starting on Celebration Hill, so Bianka herded Serenity and Dorthea toward the tram. She settled on the seat and put Serenity on her lap to insulate her from casual metal contact.

A trio of girls in full Lolita garb boarded after them. Each one of them dropped a curtsey to her and her mother before sitting down. The one wearing a colorful carousel on her skirt waved at Serenity and then winked at Bianka before hiding her giggle behind a lace covered hand. It was always flattering to be flirted with. It was probably her pink hair. Bianka nodded back to them and smiled as they whispered between themselves. They were cute, but not her type. The one in full goth glanced at her friends, then came over to introduce herself to Serenity.

"Hi, I'm Ariel. What's your name, Princess?"

"Seri," Serenity answered with a bright smile. They shook hands formally. Ariel settled on the seat next to them as the tram started to move.

"Hi, Seri. Is this your first time at the zoo?"

"No, I love animals." Serenity smiled at the young woman but leaned back against her mother and a back towards her grandmother. Little alarm bells started again. Was this social anxiety? Or was it just the fact that the little goth was wearing a lot of clanging bangles. AKA common sense.

"Me too. My favorites are bats, obviously." Ariel pointed to the little cluster of bats on her shoulder. "But I come here to see penguins and ravens too."

"I like the cats. Especially the leopard. I really want one for home, but Mom says they need more room than an apartment. Which sucks."

Ariel nodded sympathetically. "I want to keep a penguin, but my roommates," she shot a glare at her friends, "seem to think that building a pool in the middle of the living room is a bad idea."

Serenity giggled at that. Her posture was easing a bit as the conversation continued. The tram was pulling to a stop. "It was nice to meet you, Miss Ariel," Serenity said.

"And you, Miss Seri. Maybe we'll see you again around the zoo."

The Lolita's each dipped a little curtsey to Bianka as they left with a little kiss from Ariel sent in Serenity's direction. "Mom, can I get a dress like that?"

"We'll see what we can find at the thrift store to make one," Dorthea promised. "My sewing machine still works." She kissed Seri on the forehead. "Come on now, the leopards are waiting."

That was true, but first, there was the animal encounters and a host of African animals. They ran across the trio of Lolita's several times throughout the day and there was a tall male goth in all black who gave Bianka a flourished bow and a sly smile. If he hadn't been whiter than snow, she might even have flirted back.

As it was, she just smiled and gave him a nod of acknowledgement.

As they stood in the bat habitat, Bianka noticed a small, dark shadow that slid along the wall. It curled around the edge of the room and lifted one starfish like arm to wave at her. It was a baby Time Meister in the real world and Bianka pushed off the urge to cry. Now that she knew they were real, it seemed that she couldn't not see them. Damn it. Her mother didn't react, but Seri frowned at the spot as though she thought there was something there. She didn't say anything though.

Lunch was peanut butter and jelly sandwiches brought from home and a shared soda from the snack cart. The picnic area was full of running kids and tired looking parents. Serenity looked at one passing toddler with a disgust too old for her face. "I was never like that was I?"

"No, Sweetie," Bianka reassured. Because you were still in and out of the hospital, she didn't add. She'd still needed her vaccines and vaccines meant needles. Someday, Dr. Marx had promised, they would figure out how to do vaccines through hyposprays like on Star Trek. It couldn't come soon enough. Serenity's new admirers had settled down to have a picnic nearby. The three young women giggled at each other and squealed over pictures on each other's phones. The tall male goth wandered by with a bottle of water. He glanced over his shoulder at the collection of young women with an almost smile on his lips. He nodded to Bianka as he passed.

"You haven't dated in years," her mother said absently.

"I'm not interested in a relationship, Mom."

"Hmm." Dorthea dropped the topic, but her daughter eyed her suspiciously. "Otters and bats now?" she asked her grand daughter. Serenity nodded.

"And the slide?"

"We'll take a look at it. As long as it's been painted recently, it should be fine."

Serenity took the condition with as much grace as possible. She sighed over the last bites of her sandwich and apple slices. She wiped her fingers with the wet wipe her mother handed her and then pulled her gloves back on. Bianka cleared away the trash and they were off to the second part of the zoo. Bianka did her best to ignore the little shadow starfish that followed them through the area. Once, when she stood too close to the wall it had wrapped a tendril around her ankle. It was almost shy, and she didn't have the heart to kick it off, but she did step away as soon as she could justify it.

The ride home was quiet. Serenity leaned against Bianka's side. Dorthea read the zoo newsletter. In a little plastic bag emblazoned with the zoo's logo, there was a stuffed prairie dog and a tiny black bat. It had taken two hurried conversations between mother and daughter to narrow it down to just two animals. It would have been so easy to spend far too much on the outing. The bus had the familiar smell of humans in an enclosed space and the spice of someone's dinner they were bringing home.

There were two stray dogs in the alley near the apartment building. They had found a chicken carcass in the trash and were busy pulling meat off of it. She bit her lip. Chicken bones were dangerous for dogs, weren't they? Still, they weren't her dogs. She continued past them. Serenity skipped ahead a few steps and then waited for them to catch up before repeating the action. It was just a few steps, so Bianka didn't call her on it. She had started teaching her daughter self-defense at five. She'd be able to hold off the older kids long enough for Bianka to get to her side.

Dorthea sighed. "I'll stay the night, if you don't mind, dear."

"Of course not. I should probably talk to Jazz tonight. What are we going to do for dinner?"

"Soup and rice?"

"We'll have to see what's in the cupboard. I think I have a jar of chicken soup." There was one soup that came in jars as opposed to cans. Even though it had a metal top, it had proven to not have much cross-contamination and Serenity didn't react to it the way she did canned goods. She'd have to talk to Dr. Marx about finding a way to test if aluminum would be safe for her in the future. Maybe she was growing out of her sensitivity? She laughed a bit at her thoughts and shook off her mother's questioning look. "And I think there's a little ice cream left for dessert."

Chapter 27

Jasmine was behind the bar wearing a bright green headscarf when Bianka made her way into the building. She wasn't supposed to be on-shift, but she wanted to check the schedule and ask Jazz for one more favor. She settled in the corner of the bar where she'd first seen Blue. Jazz plopped a glass of water in front of her and smiled in greeting. "Give me ten to get a new round poured up."

Bianka nodded. The Monsters were playing and doing a fairly respectable job of covering a Smashing Pumpkins song. It was a new one for them. Wenceslas usually went for ruining late seventies songs. The crowd was filled with the usual hipsters at this time of the night. They were mostly drinking watered down whiskey and craft beers. She wasn't sure that most of them were old enough to remember the original song and that just made her feel old down to her bones.

Her eyes caught on a mixed group in the corner. Something about them made the bouncer part of her brain say "trouble." As she watched them though, they seemed quiet enough. The nerd in the middle of the group winced at another purposefully off note. He pinched the bridge of his nose just under his glasses and sent a pleading look at his probably significant other. His boyfriend patted his hands and grinned. Oh, it was Sean and a new group. Sean was a hard-core Monsters fan who actually stayed until the food-service set showed up and the Monsters changed to their original work. His friends were normally not that enthusiastic after the first sets.

Jazz leaned next to her. "So? How'd it go?"

"Visitation rights and her husband is an asshole. She's not drinking bottles of wine anymore though."

Jazz's eyebrows rose. "You sponsoring her?"

"No, I adopted her," she told her sponsor and best friend honestly. "But if she decides to do it, I was going to ask you to sponsor her. I can help her with her daughter's agoraphobia and PTSD, you can help her with the drinking?"

"Oh, Allah, what happened to the poor girl?"

"She witnessed her brother's murder. She says that 'Outside ate him,' and freaks out about it. She had a panic attack during the custody discussion, poor thing."

"Poor baby." Jasmine nodded though. "My word on it. If she needs a sponsor, I'll take her on. Keep it in the family. Speaking of? There was a possibility of a specialist?"

"The lawyer had a name for me, I just need to get a blood sample to him."

"Have you told Seri yet?"

"That the dragon says that it's a good idea, but I need to talk to Dr. Marx."

Jasmine laughed. "I like dragon as a word for lawyer. It suits." She was called away by one of the waitresses. Bianka surveyed the bar again. The crowd mixture seemed fairly normal. A few new faces, only one of which had stereotypical black framed glasses. He seemed to be going for a Harry Potter look though, so she gave him a few mental points for trying to be slightly different.

It felt like it had been a lifetime since she was here in the middle of life. This was the place she'd found her feet and a little cobbled-together family of Jasmine and Jim and the rest of the crew. Wenceslas was like the little brother – a little spoiled and bratty – and she'd missed seeing him. She loved Blue like a daughter and Andre and Linnaeus were awesome, but it had been lonely as Hell in the time bubble. It was nice to be somewhere where time ran normally, and the streets didn't change on you.

A young man in a fairly tattered jacket was hovering near the door. Bianka smiled in welcome. It was ingrained habit. He blinked a bit at her. He offered a hesitant smile back and drifted toward the bar. He winced a bit as another off-note hit the room. He looked as thin and hungry as Rocks and Sparky. She waved down Simon and asked him to get her a bowl of nuts. He grinned at her and put them on the bar. "Don't eat them all yourself," he told her. "You'll make yourself sick and then you won't be able to throw Sean's bodyguard out later."

She laughed at him. The thin young man sat down and nibbled at the nuts she'd moved toward him. Through some contortions managed to grab him a bottle of water. He took it with what looked like awe. "Thank you, Ma'am."

"Enjoy," she told him and turned her attention back to soaking up the familiar atmosphere of the bar. Jazz rolled her eyes. "Aren't they cute?"

"They're vicious little ticks," she muttered. "Coffees all around. Like this is a Starbucks."

"If I asked you to cover for another two days?"

"So you can go visit the specialist? Of course. Unless you want someone to go with you."

She considered that for a long moment. "No, I'll be fine. I just need a couple more days. I couldn't get an appointment last week." It wasn't technically a lie. She'd tracked down the name in one of Andre's books and she'd been in the time bubble. Jasmine put a hand on Bianka's wrist. Her nails were the same color as her scarf.

"I told you a long time ago, I will help you with your baby."

"Thanks." Some tension Bianka hadn't noticed in her spine melted away. Jasmine had saved her so many times that she'd lost count. It always felt like the next time would be the one time too many. "Do you need me tonight?"

"Just as a bouncer if it comes up. If you want to slip home and spend some time with your daughter, that's fine."

"We spent the day and Mom's at the apartment. I think she's actually going to break down and move in."

"That's wonderful!" Jasmine's smile was like a neon light. It always lit up her entire face. "And I can start converting your daughter in front of her."

The idea of a Baptist versus Muslim fight over her daughter's faith made Bianka crack up. "I can't wait. I'll set up dinner soon. No pork, right?"

"Right."

"Ice cream for desert maybe. Is artificial vanilla okay?"

"I have never turned down a cookie with vanilla or not," she replied with a wink. "Anything happen while you were gone?"

"One really intense craving. I pushed through, but I had a not so good night after that. I managed to wean Blue down to three glasses from three bottles. I asked her if she thought being drunk for court would be a good idea."

"Are you going to get her to go to a meeting or three? Or thirty?"

"It will be up to her. She's all giddy because she gets to see her daughter for a long weekend."

"Speak of the devil. It's your girlfriend," Jazz teased.

Bianka turned to the door to see none other than Blue coming in. She was as glittery as ever. She scanned the crowd and lit up when she saw Bianka. She shimmied through the room and fetched up against Bianka in a one-armed hug. "I totally forgot to give you this yesterday." She handed over a business card. "I put my cell number on there so you can call me any time and my email so we can set up that playdate. I'll send someone to come pick you up," she promised. "Water?"

"Water," Bianka agreed.

"Not for me."

Jasmine laughed. "I'm Jasmine. You can call me Jazz. I hear you're part of the family now."

"That's right." Blue smiled. "Periwinkle. But you can call me Blue."

"Nice to meet you, Blue." They shook hands and the young man twitched a bit. He looked around himself a bewildered. Blue claimed a stool and ordered a sangria. A quick brow twitch from Jasmine had her supplied with the non-alcoholic version they made up from designated drivers. Blue seemed enraptured by the music and Bianka didn't take any offense.

"What's wrong, honey?" Bianka asked the young man.

"You can see me," he murmured.

Bianka digested that for a moment. "It's okay. We won't throw you out. We don't have much beyond nuts to eat, but I'll get you to the shelter if you need it."

"It's just... no one sees me. They look past me and never hear me."

"I see you." She put a hand on his arm. He was too thin and that made sense if he was living on the streets and hadn't figured out the shelters and food pantries yet. He might be using, but she wasn't sure. "And if you need help with rehab, we can call someone for you."

He shook his head. His hair was long, but it didn't seem too matted or dirty. He had found somewhere to clean up at least. Maybe one of the bathrooms in the gas station or something. His skin had a slightly chalky look though, over what would be its natural brown. "I'm clean," he promised with a wry smile. "Though sometimes it doesn't seem like a bad idea to take something."

"What's your name, honey?"

"Tom."

"Welcome to Murray's," she said. "I'm Bee."

He seemed more settled immediately. "I... If there's a shelter, I'd like to see if I can qualify. I haven't had a job in ages," he admitted.

"Let's see what we can do to get you back on your feet." Her mom would shake the church phone trees for him. They'd get him back on his feet. Maybe some new clothes to do interviews in. "First things first. Have you had a meal today?"

He shook his head.

Bianka unzipped the pocket on the lower part of her leg and pulled out a power bar. She kept them on her. It was an indulgence that she'd made peace with. "Here. Eat this. It's going to be better for you than peanuts."

"Thank you, Miss Bee," he said with a brilliant smile that showed he wasn't broken yet.

Blue glanced over at them. "Did I overhear that you're looking for a job? What's your field?" She spun around on her barstool.

"I used to do retail, but they laid me off and I haven't found anything since then."

"Tell me more."

Bianka leaned back. Jazz looked over at her and smiled. "Good job," she mouthed. Bianka did her best not to blush. Her mother hadn't managed to keep her in the church, but some of the lessons had worn off. Helping those in need had always been a hallmark of her mother's life. Even when they were strapped themselves, she'd made a point of tithing by helping at the church's shelter and food kitchen. Bianka could do no less than follow that example.

Chapter 28

"Seri, I need to get some blood to take to the specialist." Bianka put on a pair of gloves and opened her kit to pull out some capillary tubes and a ceramic knife that was set aside for the purpose. She cleaned the knife's edge.

Serenity sighed. "Can we take it from my leg?" she asked.

"I don't see why not."

"Oh good." She pulled her skirt up to expose the scar on her upper thigh that Dr. Marx usually used. Bianka cleaned it with some rubbing alcohol and let it dry. She pricked the skin and used the capillary tubes to gather three samples of blood. It was less than most doctors took, but according to Linnaeus the specialist shouldn't need a full bottle of blood. She put them into a Ziplock bag and closed it. She put a small Hello Kitty Band-Aid onto her daughter's leg and kissed just above the leg. "That's all?"

"That's all."

"Okay." Seri returned to her workbook. It was the animal section and Bianka was beginning to think that biology or veterinarian questions were going to start soon. As long as she wore latex gloves her daughter should be okay using scalpels. As long as she didn't cut herself or stick herself with a needle. Okay, time to change that idea. No panicking about situations that were ten years in the future.

Bianka stored the blood in the fridge. She couldn't leave Serenity alone. She wasn't old enough yet. That magical age was several years away. Even then, leaving her with someone other than her tutor or her grandmother was terrifying. Bianka looked around the apartment. She should clean before her mother moved in. Chappy launched himself across the room, buzzing past her face, and decided to pretend he was a hat for Serenity. He settled down and spread out his wings in a jaunty fashion. Bianka's heart returned to normal as Serenity giggled. Her "pet" was trying to kill her.

She scrubbed at the counters and opened a new trash bag to get rid of the food that had gone off over the week away. She fantasized about having magic for a moment then laughed at herself. She knew very well that magic didn't solve problems, just look at Blue or Andre. Still, not having to do the dishes would be wonderful. The phone rang. "Hello?" she answered it immediately in order to avoid the job of cleaning the kitchen.

"Hi, sweetie. I've given notice. But we need to talk about what furniture I should bring."

"Your bed is metal framed isn't it? We can wrap it with something." The conversation was surprisingly short. There wasn't a lot of furniture that her mother was attached to and there was less that wasn't mostly metal. Serenity had settled down with her plastic embroidery kit. She was making a pink and purple butterfly to give to her grandmother for Christmas. Bianka had nothing to do but get back to work. The rest of the night passed normally.

The next morning when Mrs. West got there to work through the schoolwork for the day, Bianka smiled at her. "Hello, Mrs. W."

"Did your job go well last week?"

"Yes, ma'am. We got her to the lawyer and the courthouse and stopped her husband from doing anything stupid. She's got partial visitation now."

The woman was just about ten years older than she was, but she seemed as though she was already a spinster aunt and had always been one. She just nodded at the news. "Are you staying for lessons today?"

"No, I have an appointment with a specialist."

"Good luck." West gave her an impersonal nod and went to sit down with Seri at the coffee table. She folded herself down onto the floor. Bianka shook her head at her back. Chappy launched himself across the room and settled on her shoulder.

//Dislike// he informed her. //Blind.//

Bianka didn't respond to him until she had called out a goodbye and headed out of the apartment. "She's a good teacher. Now, how do I find the market?"

//Alley.//

Bianka sighed. "Seriously? Fine," she muttered. The two stray dogs jumped up as she walked into the alley, their tails wagging. The poor things had to have just been recently abandoned to still love humans. She knelt down and held out a hand to them to sniff. They butted up under her hand for scratches behind the ear and her heart melted a little bit. She gave them a quick pet and then blinked as she noticed the ribbons around their necks. "Rocks? Sparky?" she whispered. Their tails moved double-time.

//Court.// Bianka had no clue what he was trying to say.

"Okay, so the pink-terror is planning to get me to the Market. Are you coming with me?" They both turned and stood -- one to either side -- like bodyguards and she laughed. "That's a yes, I guess." The alley was just as dirt and trash filled as usual. It was late enough in the day that the two homeless men who lived in the alley had gone out looking for food or cash or whatever else they did during the day.

//Forward,// Chappy ordered. He rubbed his front paws together, like a little mastermind. The alley seemed to shift half-way through it. The colors became sharper, louder, and a hum started to build in her ears. Then, there was a pop and suddenly the air was filled with the smells of cooking meat and the sound of multiple people talking. There was the clank of a blacksmith to the left of them and she could see a man dressed in a full rainbow patchwork outfit playing a flute surrounded by a horde of smiling faces.

Sparky and Rocks transformed into the long lanky humans she knew them as. They still wore her ribbon around their throats as ties. "Hello, Miss," Sparky said. "Going to meet someone?"

"Andre told me about a healer who might be able to help my daughter." She was quiet when she told him. Andre had also warned her about letting people hear real names. Given that changing Blue's name had made it impossible for people to track her, she was inclined to believe it.

"Rocks and me would be happy to walk with you," Sparky informed her. "Unless you need something else we could help with?"

"No, just finding this person quickly would be best. I need to be home in time to make dinner."

"Right then," Rocks said. "Let me find this healer for you."
Bianka fished a piece of parchment out of her pocket and handed
it to him. He looked at the name and then frowned at the street for
a while. She looked at Sparky, but he seemed content to wait, so
she stood quietly and let the spectacle swirl around her. The
occasional passing individual dipped a curtsey to her, and she
nodded at them with a professional half-smile. The old woman
who had given her the ribbon wandered by and gave her a
toothless smile.

"Good for you, luv," she said. She patted her arm and then
left. She disappeared a moment later. Sparky looked at her with
awe on his face.

"What?"

"You know Lady Fate?"

"Know? Not really. She gave me some ribbon."

"Gave? Wow," Rocks' jaw dropped. He shook himself. "This
way, Miss."

Bianka raised a brow but followed him into the Market.
"You can find anyone?"

"Hellhounds are good at finding people," he told her with a
self-satisfied smile. "And turning invisible." She smiled at his
obvious pride and followed him through the market. The wildness
– the life of the place – was so different from the time bubble. It
was a confusion of noise and light and a press of humans, but
everyone seemed to be enjoying themselves. She was sure that
there were homeless, addicts, and thieves mixed in with the rest
of the crowd, but they were hidden in the shadows cast by the
flashing lights of the street performers. She managed to avoid the
showers of glitter-red from the stage magician performing on the
corner. She narrowed her eyes at him, and he smiled an apology at
her.

Then, they were out of the arena of spectacle and into the
quieter business streets with lawyers and printmakers and dusty
old bookshops with leaning towers that might have the answers
she needed. Two streets further on and they had passed into the
medical area. There was an actual snake oil salesman cutting a
live snake into his boiling brew on one side and what looked to be
a state of the art surgical practice on the other. They forced their
way past crowded streets of hopeful people with canes and
crutches and a small woman in a mechanical chair that walked like

a tired elephant and looked like it was held together with bailing wire and good wishes.

Then, Rocks stopped in front of a tidy Tudor style house with a door that almost came to Bianka's chest. It had cheerful red gardenias in the window-boxes. The wooden sign above the door read "Professor Goldbug's Cures and Curses." Bianka steeled her nerves and knocked on the door. You will not react to whatever is behind that door, she told herself.

"Come in! Come in!" a cheerful voice called out. Bianka opened the door and tucked herself through it as though she were crawling into a play-structure with her daughter. Rocks followed her in, wearing his dog shape and Sparky stayed by the door. He leaned against the outside wall with his arms crossed and a frown on his face as he watched the crowd.

Inside was a cozy sitting room with a deep purple carpet and child-sized chairs. Bianka resigned herself to sitting on the floor. Professor Goldbug was no more than three feet tall with the rich brown skin that reminded her of freshly turned earth. His eyes were shimmering gold as were the wings that jutted out and to the sides. They flapped excitedly as he saw her. "Just a minute. Just a minute. Let me change the chairs for you!" He wove his fingers in an intricate pattern and half of the room sized up to suit her.

Bianka sat down on one of the chairs which had been sized up for her. Rocks settled at her feet; eyes trained on the Professor. She wasn't sure what his species was. She assumed he was a fairy and therefore someone to be careful of. "Professor Goldbug?" she asked.

"Yes, milady." He smiled broadly showing just a few too many teeth, but it didn't seem like a threat.

"Lawyer Draconis gave me your name. He said that you might be able to help me with a medical issue my daughter has."

Goldbug settled in a chair and folded his hands in his lap. "I'd love to help. Tell me what the matter is."

"What is the going rate for your consultation?" she asked. She'd been burned by medical bills before.

"First consultation is always free," he told her, nodding seriously. "If there's a treatment plan or follow-up, then we can determine payment."

"Agreed. And you'll clearly define when we start developing treatments or performing any tests which are not considered part of your consultation."

Goldbug's wings fluttered a bit. "Yes, agreed." His voice grew a little sharper.

"My daughter is allergic to metal."

The wings went still and Goldbug stretched his body forward toward her. Rocks' ears pricked forward and his head lifted from his paws. "Your daughter's parentage is?"

"She's half fairy," Bianka confirmed.

Goldbug hummed. "Yes, I've seen that before. Normally, they don't survive past the first year," he told her bluntly. "You wouldn't be here if she were that young. How old is your daughter?"

"Seven."

His eyes widened. "Seven? Truly?" He stood up and started pacing. "But you live on the Outside. How extraordinary!" He tapped a finger on his lips. "She has a doctor?"

"Yes. He has come up with some work-arounds, but no cure."

"No. No. I wouldn't expect that." He muttered to himself for a few minutes as he wandered back and forth. "You'll need something that your doctor can verify." His wings fluttered in time with his feet. "And treatment that can work Outside."

He paused. "I believe that I can help you," he said, after he looked at her for a long moment. "My price for the tests will be the right to publish the study on your daughter's treatment in my book about halflings."

"And the treatment plan proposal?"

"No fee for the proposal. Your Hellhound will act as witness to that. I will need a vial of blood to test."

"I have a capillary tube of blood. Will that suffice?"

Goldbug considered. "I may need more later."

"If I show it to you, can you give me a more concrete answer as to how much blood you'll require?"

"Yes."

Bianka removed one capillary tube of blood. He peered at it through a jeweler's loop that he conjured from somewhere. Bianka thought it was likely from his pocket but didn't want to assume.

"I would need one more of these tubes," he said finally.

"To summarize: two of these tubes as the price of testing. A free treatment proposal for me to take to my doctor Outside. And the rights to write about my daughter's treatments, whether or not they are successful, in payment for the treatments themselves."

"Agreed," Prof. Goldbug said with a firm nod.

"Agreed," she responded. "Rocks here will act as our witness." She handed over two tubes of blood.

"Excellent. I will need about two hours."

Bianka looked at her watch. "I will be back in two hours as marked by my watch, Professor Goldbug." she said. "Come on, Rocks. There were bookstores out there."

"In two hours, Queen Bee," he replied, absently, eyes already on the blood.

Rocks stayed in his dog form as Sparky pushed off from the wall and joined her. "I need to be back in two hours," Bianka told him. "Let's go check out one of the bookstores."

"Sure, ma'am." The bookstore had dusty windows and stacks of book that were too high to see over. It smelled like the old library she'd hidden away in as a child – mildew in the corners and dusty books that no one cared about. She trailed her fingers over the spines as she peered at the titles. Most of them she couldn't read, but there was one she recognized from Andre's library. She studied the stack, then took the chance to remove the book in one quick motion. The stack above wobbled as it settled down, but it didn't fall. She flipped through the book carefully. It seemed to be an older copy of the book. There was writing in the margins in faded blue ink.

"Can I help you, milady?" The man was nearly bent in half, leaning on his cane. His hair was a wreath of wispy white around his head. He peered up at her with sharp blue eyes.

"What's the price of this book?" She offered the book for him to take, but he waved it away.

"Woman's book." He twisted his lips for a moment as he studied her. "One day's earnings."

She considered that. It would mean it was about eighty dollars, with a good tips night. She flipped through it one more time, then dug in her pocket for cash. She'd brought enough to cover a doctor's visit and possible lab work. That the blood was enough for the testing meant she could afford to splurge on the book of magic that she'd fallen in love with. She handed the folded money to the old man.

He blinked. "Feel free to stop back any time. I will put woman books aside for you."

"If I'm this way again, I'll try to stop by." She didn't want to promise anything. She didn't think she'd be able to give up the Market now that she knew she could get to it easily, but that didn't mean she'd be able to find his store again.

"B?" a familiar voice said from the door. She turned to see Linnaeus.

"Lin!" She greeted him with a kiss to the cheek. "How have you been?" He drew her into the street.

"Well. All three of us are. You're invited to the Naming Ceremony," he told her. "I've sent the invitation along to Blue, but I'm so glad that I managed to see you."

"Thank you for inviting me. Unless there's something happening with Seri, I will be there."

Linnaeus nodded. "You're welcome to bring her as well. I'd love to meet her." He frowned. "Though that might not be safe. I don't know how strong the illusion is."

"I'll discuss it with her. She may want to come, even if she has to be fully covered. Who would miss seeing your baby?" She tucked her arm through his offered arm, and he led her away to a coffee shop she hadn't seen. They chatted until Sparky cleared his throat.

"Time to get going so's we can get back, miss."

"Thank you, Sparky. I'm sorry, Lin, I've got an appointment."

"It was lovely to see you. No, let me get the coffee, dearheart." He kissed her hands. "You take good care of your little one and we'll compare notes on child-rearing when you come back and I've lost what little sanity I've left." She laughed at that, kissed his cheek in farewell and let Sparky lead her back to Professor Goldbug.

Chapter 29

Dr Marx's office was cold, as usual. It was strange to be in a mostly white, brightly lit space after the cozy confines of Goldbug's little Tudor house. It had been nearly a month since she'd last been to see him and she's passed his treatment plan on to Dr. Marx. He'd needed a few weeks to review the plan. Bianka pulled her denim jacket around her a little more. She was turning into her mother – needing a sweater everywhere these days -- despite the fact that her hair was properly bright pink. Dr. Marx was running late, even though she was there after hours. Since she wasn't technically a paying patient, he wasn't obligated to make it to their appointment on time, but still, it would have been nice. She had to get to work by seven to set up the bar. The pediatrician showed up with his hair sticking up like a mad scientist and an apologetic grin.

"I know it's been Ms. Freeman, but I just got word. Is 'Your majesty' more appropriate or do you prefer Queen Bee?"

Bianka narrowed her eyes at him. "What the heck are you talking about?"

He gestured at her shoulder as though there were a military ranking there. "Word just got to me and I want to apologize for not recognizing your rank. Princess Serenity hasn't had an incident, has she?"

"No, she's been okay. Rocks and Sparky have been making sure she's safe. But what are you talking about rank? I'm just Bianka. The bartender. Remember? My daughter's got a weird allergy and you're testing the possible solution I brought you before we let her take it. Any of this ringing a bell?" Bianka was frowning now. Had someone done something to him? Was someone mad that she'd adopted Blue?

"You don't know." He stared at her, his dark eyes full of something like wonder. "You really don't know. You're a queen. A full on, acknowledged by all four of the original courts queen."

"Let's talk about Seri first and then we'll come back to the fact that you are apparently either the same species as my ex or mixed race like my daughter."

"The solution you brought me, it won't work. Not the way they said it would at least. This is not a one and done cure for the metal allergy."

Bianka slumped in the horribly uncomfortable Lucite chair. The first time she'd been in the office, they'd been horribly uncomfortable leather and metal contraptions. He'd gotten rid of them when he found out that Seri was allergic to metal. Seeing the plastic chairs had made her break down in tears. It had taken twenty minutes, and the patient soothing of his nurse to get back under control. He'd always been honest that he didn't think Seri would live to be an adult. "But?" she prompted.

"But I think we're closer to a cure than we've ever been. And it was probably worth any price to get our hands on it. You did the right thing. Even if you had to sacrifice a goat or something."

"Two capillary tubes of Seri's blood," she stated. "But it will be a cure at some point?"

"Yes. I think we can at least start an exposure program without worrying about anaphylaxis anymore. And I'm confident that we can manufacture this here on common commercial equipment like any other formulary!" He digressed into medical technobabble for a minute and Bianka nodded encouragingly. She remembered a lot from her chemistry classes, but she was not a medical researcher. The doctor had been taking care of Serenity for more than seven years now and hadn't asked more of her than she could give. He wound down with a proud smile.

"I'm glad," Bianka said. "I'm glad that this wasn't wasted. That it will actually do something and that I won't have to go back to the same vendor to get more of it. We'll have to talk about the next step with Seri in a minute, but I'm dying to know why you think I'm a queen. Has my mother been telling you stories? She used to call me Queen Bee."

"As you might have already guessed, I'm mixed like your daughter." He sat back in his chair and gestured with his reading glasses. "I don't have nearly as much of the blood in my system though. It's my grandmother who's related to the Winter court. I have enough to see magic and magic creatures and enough status in the Outside to get all the good gossip from my cousins. And you, my lady, are the number one topic of gossip. No one's really sure what your powers are, where you came from, or what your preferred tokens are."

He leaned forward with an eager smile – like she was one of his research projects. "When did you get crowned?"

She opened her mouth to deny it, then closed her mouth after a breath. "I don't know exactly when," she said finally. "Are you serious about this?"

"Yes, they said that your first official action was adopting a fairy?" He raised his brows.

"It was an accident. But I'm her sponsor now, at the very least."

He nodded. "She had a drinking problem? You found her at the bar?"

"She found me. She needed help getting to see her daughter and her lawyer, and I couldn't turn her down when she asked me to be her chaperone."

"And you managed to adopt her? Did the lawyer help?"

Bianka shook her head and smiled. "Okay, I'd love to go into the whole story, but I have a shift tonight and I can't be late after Jasmine's been covering my shift for a week and a half already. What do I need to do with Seri?"

The man narrowed his eyes are her. "First, you need to accept me as a member of your court, and then we'll schedule an appointment."

"As a member of my court. Really?"

"Really. And tell the pink Xetius over there that he can't eat my plant."

"Chappy!" She sighed. He must have hidden in her pocket to follow her. She went to collect the pink hamster-moth. As soon as she picked him up, he fluttered from her hand to her cleavage. "Letch."

//Affirmative.//

"Sorry about the plant."

"Shouldn't be any lasting damage. Now, about a symbol that's yours. Black ribbon?"

Bianka sighed. She dug a pair of small scissors and a roll of black ribbon out of the pocket of her black cargo pants. She cut off a length of ribbon and shaped it into a two headed version of an awareness campaign. "I hereby accept Dr. Marx as a member of my court." She tacked the ribbon onto his tie with the little Mickey Mouse tie tack he always wore when Serenity wasn't scheduled to be in the room.

He nodded sharply. "Thank you, milady. Now, about seeing Serenity next week. What day is best for you? I want to talk to her about what the possible side effects could be before we proceed."

Bianka chewed at her lip. "Wednesday? It's slow at the bar and usually around here too according to Lydia." Lydia was Dr. Marx's main assistant. She scheduled appointments, gossiped about celebrities with clients, and always had hard candies on her desk that looked like she'd stolen them from her grandmother.

"Lydia is totally human by the way," he told her. "And you still haven't told me about your coronation." He pulled up his calendar on the tablet he kept on his desk. "Yes, Wednesday should be perfect. I'll see the two of you starting at 3?"

"We'll be here," she promised. "And we'll set an appointment as adults to go out and get some coffee to talk about fantasy stories."

He grinned at her.

Chapter 30

Serenity gripped her mother's hand as the car pulled to a smooth stop in front of them. It was a nice car. The kind Bianka had always wanted, as opposed to Blue's vehicle. It had what looked like a fleet tag on it, so Bianka assumed it was from her company. "Miss B, Blue thought you'd like a familiar face." Tom smiled at her. His skin didn't look chalky anymore and he was wearing jeans and a tee-shirt that didn't look like they should be used to clean up the barroom floor.

"Tom! I'm glad to see you. I knew Blue had found you a job. This is my daughter Serenity."

"Hello, Princess," he greeted. He shook her hand solemnly. "What a lovely dress."

"Thank you."

"Is there a booster?"

Tom nodded. "Blue said she's made it safe."

They settled Serenity in the booster seat before doing up the seatbelt. Serenity bore it with surprising grace, though she was obviously wishing for the day when she wouldn't need it. She pulled at the seatbelt strap. Bianka settled in the seat next to her. Tom started them off. "So, what are you up to these days?"

"Blue has me writing sales copy and I love it. She likes my turns of phrase. And my retro style." She couldn't see him rolling his eyes, but she was pretty sure she could hear his amusement. "Thank you for helping me, by the way. I don't think I'd have made it much longer."

"I'm sure you'd have found a shelter," she told him firmly. "How far out does Blue live anyway?"

"Cantonville. Only about 20 minutes."

They chatted idly for the rest of the ride, Serenity chiming in asking questions. She was picking at her gloves, which Bianka knew was her nerves. The house they pulled up to seemed to be nothing spectacular. It was like the rest of the houses in the neighborhood with a brick walkway leading up to a white and black colonial house. Serenity's eyes opened wide. She'd never had a friend who lived in a house like this. To be honest, neither had Bianka. Blue was waiting for them at the door by the time they got up the front steps. Tom waved at them before taking the car back to wherever it lived.

She greeted Bianka with a hug. She knelt down to greet Serenity. "Hi. I'm Periwinkle, but you can call me Blue."

"Hello, Miss Blue," Serenity said politely, as though greeting one of the ladies at church.

"Please come in. My home is your home." The house was decidedly normal inside. To Bianka's practiced eye, there was no metal to be worried by. Everything was arts and crafts style or earlier in the visible rooms. And the decorations where wooden, glass, or plastic.

"Thank you, Blue."

"Gloriosa," Blue called. "Come meet Serenity."

Gloriosa peeked out from the dining room where she had a puzzle spread out on the table. She might have been nine, but she didn't seem to have actually outgrown her fear of strangers. Well, it was something she and Seri could work on. When she saw that Serenity was a little girl too, her posture relaxed. She came over with a big smile. "I'm Gloriosa,"

"Serenity." The two girls glanced at their mothers.

"Why don't you show Serenity around the house? You can introduce her to Mr. Teddy," Blue suggested.

Gloriosa offered her hand and the two girls left the room with more decorum than Bianka had ever managed as a kid. "Thank you, Blue. The house is lovely."

"And safe. I'm not actually bound by human constraints, so there's nothing here that should be able to hurt her. I've even stored away all of the jewelry, just in case. It's in my room and Glori knows not to go in there. Come on, I've got sweet tea for you and," she paused, "and fake sangria for me. Jasmine told me how to make it."

Bianka gave her a tight hug. Blue squeaked a bit, then laughed. "Yes, yes," she patted Bianka's back, "I'm going to talk to Jasmine about stopping drinking. I promise."

"Thank you. I'm so happy."

"Come on, Mom. Let's drink. And we'll figure out lunch. And hope we don't hear any screaming or crashes."

The kitchen was warm and lovely with brick, tile, and wood. There were open shelves full of sparkling clean glass and hand-thrown pottery. It was surprisingly free of glitter or shiny things. Sweet tea in a blown glass pitcher that looked like a bubble. "So, I do have something to ask you about."

There was a crash, followed immediately by Serenity calling out "We're okay! Nothing's broken!"

The mothers exchanged a glance and then carefully put down their drinks before bolting up the stairs. Blue took the lead because she knew the house. They found the two girls in Gloriosa's room. It was a confection of purple and lace. The trunk full of clothes was on its side, spilling out clothes. The crash has been the trunk falling off of the legs of a luggage stand. There was a one-step stepstool that was pushed to the side. The girls were fine.

"Let's get that back on its stand."

"Does it need the stand?"

"Keeps the bottom strong when it gets full of cloth." Blue settled the stand. She put the trunk back into place.

"So, what happened?" Bianka looked at her daughter.

"We tried to open the chest without the stool, and it fell over."

"Just be careful. I don't want either of you smooshed." Bianka smoothed a hand over Serenity's head.

Gloriosa looked up at her. "Are you really my grandmother now?"

"Well, I did adopt your Mom, so yes."

Serenity blinked at them. Bianka had tried to explain that she had adopted Blue, but Serenity just didn't understand. "So, I have a big sister, like you have Auntie Annie?" Bianka had two older siblings. Annie and Bart. They were old enough that they could be her parents, so it was a fair enough comparison. Bianka had been a surprise baby.

"Yes."

"You don't have to think of me as your sister, if you don't want to."

Serenity considered. "Can I call you Auntie Blue?"

"Yes, of course you can," Blue told her. "And Glori, you can call Bianka, Auntie Bee, if you want."

Bianka nodded. "I'd be happy to be Auntie Bee."

The two girls seemed to consider things for a minute. Then, they both nodded. "Okay. Can we still play dress up?"

"Of course. Just be careful not to drop the trunk on yourselves and call if you need help," Bianka told her daughter. Blue dropped a kiss on Gloriosa's forehead. Despite the fact that she was two years older than Serenity, she wasn't much bigger or more mature than Serenity. Bianka assumed it was due to the differences in Underhill. Or maybe it was just that Serenity had confronted her death and acted older than herself. She and Blue retreated. They hovered in the hall until they heard the girls starting to develop an elaborate play involving dragons and stone giants and a princess in a tower.

The sweet tea and fruit-juice sangria seemed to be just the ticket. "I'm going to call for pizza for lunch and if the girls are lucky, we'll leave some for them," Blue stated. "And I need candy. I think my heart is still beating double-time."

"Here's to keeping them alive and intact."

"So, mote it be," Blue said, clinking her glass against Bianka's.

"So, mote it be," Bianka echoed. She felt a brief flair of warmth on her skin. Maybe her mom was right, and it was time to start dating again, if she was blushing from a toast with Blue.

But right now, her daughters were safe and that's all she really wanted.

The End

www.ingramcontent.com/pod-product-compliance
Lightning Source LLC
Chambersburg PA
CBHW051251170626
46809CB00004B/1593